Danger Lies Ahead

Danger Lies Ahead

Paul McCusker

PUBLISHING
Colorado Springs, Colorado

DANGER LIES AHEAD
Copyright © 1995 by Focus on the Family.
All rights reserved. International copyright secured.

Library of Congress Cataloging-in-Publication Data
McCusker, Paul, 1958–
    Danger lies ahead / Paul McCusker.
       p.   cm.—(Adventures in Odyssey ; 7)
    Summary: Jack finally turns to his parents, who teach him about trust and friendship,
after the new kid at school has ensnared him in a web of lies.
    ISBN 1-56179-369-8
    [1. Friendship—Fiction.   2. Family life—Fiction.   3. Christian life—Fiction.]
I. Title.   II.   Series: McCusker, Paul, 1958–
Adventures in Odyssey ; 7.
PZ7.M47841635Dan   1995
[Fic]—dc20   95-7714
                                                  CIP
                                                  AC

Published by Focus on the Family Publishing, Colorado Springs, CO 80995.

Distributed in the U.S.A. and Canada by Word Books, Dallas, Texas.

Editor: Gwen Weising
Designer: Bradley Lind
Cover Illustration: Jeff Haynie

Printed in the United States of America

95 96 97 98 99 00/10 9 8 7 6 5 4 3 2 1

For Donald, Genesis, and Joe
Thanks for the inspiration

*Fans of the audio and video series
of **Adventures in Odyssey** may wonder why some
of their favorite characters aren't found in these
novels. The answer is simple: the novels take
place in a period of time prior
to the audio or video series.*

CHAPTER ONE

Three things happened the first day of school. Mark Prescott left Odyssey. An inmate escaped from the Connellsville Detention Center. And I met Colin Francis. Okay, maybe I'd better take things one at a time.

My name's Jack. Jack Davis. I live in a town called Odyssey. Somebody once told me it's called Odyssey because the guys who discovered it said it's a town you "oughta see." It's a pretty nice place to live if you like being able to get from your house to the center of town in 20 minutes—on your bike, that is. Which means it isn't as exciting as a big city, I guess, but I kind of like it here. Anyway, back to the three things that happened on the first day of school.

The first one I saw for myself. Oscar—he's my friend— and I walked to school past Mark Prescott's house. There was a big green moving van parked out front, and two large, hairy men in gray overalls were loading gigantic boxes. I heard one of the men yell, "That's the last crate," and then he spat on the ground like it put a period at the end of his sentence.

Oscar slowed down and tugged at my sleeve. "Look, Jack. There's Patti," he half-whispered. "What's she doing here?"

I craned my neck to look around Oscar, which isn't easy since he's kind of roly-poly and always seems to be in the way when I try to see things. I'm not saying he's fat. He just has a chunky body, which my mom says goes perfectly with his brown hair and freckles. (Moms say that kind of thing.)

"Where?" I asked, still ducking and dodging around Oscar.

Oscar pointed to the open garage. "There! See?"

I did. Patti Eldridge stood just inside with her head hung down so that I couldn't see most of her face behind the brim of her baseball cap. Her hands were shoved deep in her jeans pockets. She looked like she had just lost her best friend. Well, maybe I should say she looked like she was *about to lose* her best friend. All the kids knew that Patti and Mark Prescott had hung around together all summer after Mark moved to Odyssey. I don't know the whole story about why Mark moved here, but I think his parents were going to get a divorce. Mark moved with his mom to his grandmother's house in Odyssey. He hated it at first but got to be friends with Patti. Then his parents decided to get back together, so Mark and his mom were packing all their things up so they could move back to Washington, D. C., where they'd come from. But like I said, I don't know the whole story about that.

Patti lifted her head to look at Mark. She was crying. Mark

kicked at a trash can and said something to her just as his mom and dad came out. His dad said it was time to go. Mark's mom hugged Patti, and his dad put a hand on her shoulder. I guess Patti isn't a huggy kind of girl, because she suddenly jumped on her bike and pedaled away like crazy. She nearly knocked Oscar and me over. I could hear her sniffling and sobbing as she went past.

I glanced back at Mark and his parents. Mark had moved down the driveway and looked as if he was going to run after her. But he didn't. Just then he saw us and stopped dead in his tracks. I think he was crying, too. He turned around slowly and got into the backseat of a boxy, white rent-a-car.

"That was sad," Oscar said as we headed on to Odyssey Elementary School.

"Sad?" I said. "Are you kidding? The lucky kid! He gets out of the first day of school!"

*****

I didn't hear about the second event—the escaped convict—until all us kids met on the basketball blacktop for assembly. We had to get into lines for our classes before we marched into the building. Oscar and I scouted around for the sixth-grade line and knew we'd found it when we saw the bully, Joe Devlin, pushing his way to the front of the line.

"Joe's back for another try at sixth grade," I said to Oscar.

"Another chance for him to beat us up like always," Oscar said.

"I wonder how old he'll get before they decide to promote him?" I asked.

"Probably older than the teachers," Oscar answered.

Lucy Cunningham-Schultz stood at the end of the line. She was hanging onto her notebooks and shivering.

"Hey, Lucy," I said. Normally I'm not real friendly with girls, but Lucy is different from the others. She knows how to talk about things that boys like. I think it's because she wants to be a reporter when she grows up.

Lucy twirled around and looked at me through her big owl-like glasses. Her mousy hair was sticking up in different places as if she had combed it with an electric brush. Her teeth chattered as she said, "Hi, Jack. Hi, Oscar."

"Are you cold?" Oscar asked her.

"A little bit. It's chillier than I thought it'd be."

"Ha! This is a heat wave!" I said, even though it really wasn't very warm. It was kind of chilly, in fact, but you have to play things tough so people won't think you're a sissy.

"You wanna put on my jacket?" Oscar offered. He wasn't very good at playing things tough.

"Thanks," Lucy said as Oscar helped her put it on.

I rolled my eyes. I had a long way to go to teach Oscar the ways of the world.

"I guess you heard about the escaped convict," Lucy said.

"Escaped convict?" Oscar gulped.

"Cool! What escaped convict?" I asked.

"The one who got away from the Connellsville Detention

Center last night. Everybody's talking about it. It was on a special news bulletin this morning and everything!" Lucy answered. "I think they said he's armed and dangerous."

"Wow!" I said. I wondered how escaped convicts got armed after being in jail, but I imagined he'd knocked out one of the guards and stolen his gun. Or maybe he had a stash of weapons hidden away by his partner.

Oscar looked nervous as he asked, "He wasn't headed for Odyssey, was he?"

Lucy shrugged. "I don't know," she said. "They didn't say where he was going."

I punched Oscar in the arm. "If they knew which way he was headed, they'd put up a roadblock and catch him! Don't you know anything?"

Oscar said that maybe the convict was sneaking through the woods somewhere. Maybe the woods behind the school!

"Maybe he was watching us even at that minute!" Lucy added.

"Cut it out, Lucy," I said. "You're gonna make Oscar break out in hives."

The bell rang, and we whistled the theme to *Indiana Jones* as we marched into the school.

*****

The third thing happened after we had a first-day-of-school assembly in the cafeteria and Mrs. Biedermann handed out our school books before leading us to the classroom. I rounded the corner, headed for the door, and bumped into a skinny, blond-headed kid. Our books went flying.

"Watch where you're going!" the kid yelped.

"Watch where *you're* going," I said.

We stooped to pick up our books, and the kid frowned at me with watery eyes. I thought maybe I'd hurt him, so I said, "Are you new here? I haven't seen you before."

"Why do you want to know?" the kid asked.

"Just wondering," I answered. "Who are you?"

"Who are *you*?"

"I asked you first," I said. This kid obviously didn't know the rules around our school.

After picking up all the books we'd dropped, we stood up. The kid glanced around like he thought someone might be listening in. "My name's Colin Francis," he said.

"Oh. Well, I'm Jack Davis," I said.

He looked at me like he wasn't sure whether to believe me. "Jack Davis?"

"Yeah."

"So . . . what do you want?" Colin Francis asked.

"Huh?"

He squinted his eyes at me. "What do you want? Why are you telling me your name?"

"How are people gonna know who you are unless you tell them your name?" I asked. I didn't understand this kid at all, and I was getting bugged. "Look, forget it. I was just trying to be friendly."

"Sure you were," he said as if he didn't believe me.

I started to answer but stopped myself. I didn't know what to say. It was the first time I had ever felt like I needed to prove I was trying to be friendly.

I was glad when Mrs. Biedermann told us to take our seats.

*****

I sat down next to Oscar. "What about that kid?" he asked.

"I'll tell you later," I whispered.

Mrs. Biedermann stood at the blackboard and said the kinds of things teachers always say on the first day of school. She told us her name and explained that we had to fill out a bunch of forms for her files, that she expected us to do our best this year, and . . . I looked around the classroom and wondered if the guy who designed it made a lot of money. It looked like every class-room in every school in every town in every part of the world— from the flag to the pictures of the presidents to the cut-out let-ters on the bulletin board to the portable coat closet that sat on wheels in the corner to the metal desks and hard chairs.

I must have been daydreaming, because suddenly all the students were opening their books. I looked around, not sure what we were doing.

"Page three in the social studies book," Oscar whispered. Somehow he always knew when I wasn't paying attention.

I pulled my books out of the desk and sighed. Summer was over. I really was back in school. Classroom assignments, math, English, history, science, and homework were all I had to look forward to. Count on it. Nothing interesting was going to happen between now and the end of the year.

I shuffled through my stuff and soon realized I had *two* social studies books. *Weird*, I thought. *How did that happen?* And then I remembered the juggling act I did with Colin and *his* books.

"Excuse me, Mrs. Biedermann," I heard Colin say.

"Yes, Colin?"

"I'd *like* to turn to page three, but *Jack* stole my book," he said.

I couldn't believe my ears.

"Oh?" Mrs. Biedermann asked.

"I didn't *steal* his book," I said.

"Look," Colin said as he pointed, "he has two over there."

"Jack?" Mrs. Biedermann asked in a tone that meant she wanted me to explain.

"Yeah, I have two books . . ." I started to say, but Colin interrupted.

"See? And one of them is mine."

"You *know* it's yours," I said. Well, I guess I shouted. "Our books got mixed up when you bumped into me and we dropped them."

"When *you* bumped into *me*," Colin said.

"I didn't bump into you, *you* bumped into *me*," I said.

"That's enough," Mrs. Biedermann said.

"It was just an excuse to take my book," Colin went on.

"What!" I said.

"Just give him the book and we'll forget the whole thing," Mrs. Biedermann said, walking toward me.

"I didn't steal his book," I said.

Colin yelled, "Yes, you did!"

And then I told him he'd better shut up, and he told me I was just picking on him because he was the new kid at school, and I said he was lying because I didn't *care* that he was the new kid, and he yelled something back at me about being a Neanderthal, and I yelled something back at him about his family at the zoo, and Mrs. Biedermann told us both to sit down and be quiet, and we both yelled something at her . . . and that's when she sent us to the principal's office.

CHAPTER TWO

T his is a bad start, boys, a bad start," Mr. Felegy, our principal, said as he sat behind his desk and shook his head.

Colin sat in the visitor's seat next to me. I glared at him, hoping Mr. Felegy would pick up the idea that I was bugged because it was *Colin's* fault that we got in trouble. Colin sat with his hands folded in his lap and looked calmly at Mr. Felegy.

Who in the world is this kid? I wondered. *Calls me a thief, gets in trouble on his first day in a new school, and then sits like he's waiting for a bus. It doesn't make sense.*

"I'm especially surprised at *you*, Jack," Mr. Felegy said.

"Me?"

"Is this any way to welcome a new student to our school?"

"But, but, but . . ." I sounded like an outboard motor as my mouth got stuck.

"Listen to me, *both* of you," Mr. Felegy went on. "This is it. Your quota for the year."

I asked him what a quota was.

"Four of 'em make a gallon," Colin said.

"Oh," I said and wondered why Mr. Felegy was bringing up milk at a time like this.

Mr. Felegy rubbed his very high forehead. "A quota means you've used up all of your visits to me," he said. "No more trips to my office for the rest of the year or you'll be in *big* trouble. Got it?"

"Yes, sir," Colin said.

"Yes, sir," I said, too.

Mr. Felegy waved at us like he was shooing flies. "Go back to class," he ordered. *"And no more fighting."*

I stood up and walked out of his office. A phone rang, and Mrs. Stewart, the secretary, picked it up as I passed her desk. "Yes, Officer Quinn," she said into the phone, "Mr. Felegy is right here. Hold on." She cupped her hand over the mouthpiece and shouted to Mr. Felegy that Officer Quinn from the police department was on the phone.

Probably about the escaped convict, I figured. I imagined him sneaking around the school building and peeking in at the windows. I wanted to hang around to see if there was any big news, but Mrs. Stewart frowned at me, so I left.

In the hallway, Colin suddenly came up to my side. Just before we passed the big bicycle-safety bulletin board, he said, "Are you mad at me?"

"What do you think?" I answered. "I don't guess you have a lot of friends if this is how you act on your first day in a new school."

Colin nodded. "You're right. I don't have very many friends. It's because my family moves a lot."

"How come you move so much?" I asked.

"I'm not allowed to say," he said.

"Why not?"

"Because it's . . . it's a secret."

"Why is it such a big secret?" I asked, though I didn't think it could be *that* big a secret.

"If I told you, then it wouldn't be a secret," he answered.

"Yeah, sure," I said in my best I-don't-believe-a-word-you're-saying voice, and then I changed the subject. "So what's the idea of saying I stole your book when you knew it was just a mix-up?"

"When you've lived the kind of life I've lived," Colin said, "you become suspicious of everyone."

"You're only in sixth grade! What kind of life could you have lived already?"

"I can't tell you."

"Yeah, yeah, it's a big secret," I said. We were almost to the door of our classroom.

When we stopped to open the door, Colin turned to me and said, "*If* we become friends, I'll tell you *everything*."

"Fat chance," I answered with a laugh. "Why would I wanna be your friend after you got me in trouble?"

"You wanna be my friend because you wanna *know* my secrets," he said.

"Ha!" I said.

But as I sat down at my desk, I thought, *Any kid who acts this weird* must *have something interesting going on.*

*****

The rest of the morning, we did some math and wrote a paper about what we had done that summer. At lunch, Oscar, Lucy, and I sat together in the cafeteria. Like every lunch last year in school, Oscar complained about the bologna sandwich his mom had made for him. She always put tomatoes and lettuce on it, and Oscar hated that stuff. Lucy lectured him about eating vegetables. I zoned out and looked around the room. Colin was still in the food line with his tray.

I guess Lucy saw me looking at Colin, because she said, "He's kind of strange, isn't he?"

"Sort of," I said. "I sure can't figure him out."

Oscar peeled the tomato and lettuce off his sandwich and held them at arm's length like he was holding a dead skunk. "Anybody want these?" he asked.

"No, thank you," Lucy said.

"Huh uh," I said. Oscar walked over to a nearby trash can and pitched them in.

"He gives me the creeps," Lucy said, still talking about Colin.

I shrugged and said, "He doesn't give me the creeps. He just makes me wonder what he's up to."

Oscar came back from the trash can. "Maybe he's the escaped convict in disguise," he whispered loud enough for half our table to hear.

"Nah," I said. "When I was in the principal's office—"

"On the *first day of school*," Lucy reminded me.

I ignored her and resumed talking. "The phone rang, and I heard the secretary say it was Officer Quinn of the police department. He wanted to talk with Mr. Felegy about the escaped convict."

Oscar's eyes went wide. "Really? What about him?" he asked.

"Hey, it's classified stuff," I said. "Me and Ed—I mean, Mr. Felegy—gotta keep these things under our vests."

"You mean, under your hat," Lucy corrected me. "The expression is: You keep things either under your hat or close to your vest, but not under your vest."

"Thank you, Miss English Professor," I said.

Oscar looked confused. "But you're not wearing a hat, Jack. Or a vest."

"Never mind," I said, then continued real low, "but you want to be real careful today. I think the escaped convict is headed for Odyssey to get revenge on someone who testified against him at the trial. Maybe someone at this school."

"That's crazy!" Lucy said.

"I've never testified against anyone!" Oscar said as if we thought he had.

Bang!

It came out of nowhere and nearly made all of us fall off our chairs. Colin had dropped a book on the table.

"What's wrong with you?" Lucy yelled at him.

"Yeah! Are you trying to give us heart attacks?" Oscar asked.

Colin smiled at them, then at me. "I think this book is yours," he said.

"Huh?" I picked up the book. Sure enough, it was the science book I had signed out earlier in the morning. "Where'd you get this?"

"Must've picked it up by accident when we dropped our books," he said.

"I wish I'd known! I could have accused you of stealing it. Then I would have had revenge on you for saying I stole *your* book," I said, joking.

Nobody laughed. Lucy and Oscar sat there looking at Colin like he had just landed from another planet.

Colin smiled again, then said, "What makes you so sure I *didn't* steal it from you? Our desks aren't locked. Anybody could steal anything around here. This school's not very security-minded."

I tried to guess if he was serious, then decided he wasn't and chuckled to lighten the mood.

"I have to go to the library before the end of lunch," Lucy said suddenly. She grabbed her tray and left.

"You were talking about me when I walked up, weren't

you?" Colin asked.

"No way!" I said. "Why would we wanna talk about you?" I snickered as if that were the dumbest idea in the world.

"You haven't been in jail recently, have you?" Oscar asked kind of quietly.

Colin dropped onto a chair and clanged his lunch tray on the table. "What if I have?" he said. "Do you have a problem with people who've been in jail?"

"No!" Oscar said and stood up. "I was just wondering. I . . . uh. . . ."

"Where're you going, Oscar?" I asked.

"I gotta go to the library, too," he sputtered. "To . . . uh . . . check out some books and . . . stuff."

And he was gone like somebody had set his pants on fire.

"You really have a way with people, Mr. Charming," I said to Colin.

"Why did you lie to me?" Colin asked as he bit into a piece of cardboard-looking pizza.

"What are you talking about?"

Colin slowly turned and looked at me. "You said you weren't talking about me before I walked up, and you were. In fact, I'd bet a lot of money that Lucy said she doesn't like me. I probably give her the creeps."

I was surprised. "How did you know she said that?"

"Because I know people like you and Lucy," he said. "Why did you lie to me?"

"Because I didn't wanna hurt your feelings," I answered.

"Give me some credit for trying."

"You shouldn't have lied."

"What did you want me to say? 'Yeah, Colin, we were talking about you, and Lucy said you give her the creeps, and Oscar thinks you're the escaped convict in disguise.'" I felt kind of annoyed. "It's your own fault that kids don't like you. I think you set a world's record for becoming the most unpopular kid at school in the least amount of time. It's only lunch on the first day, and I'm the only one who will sit with you. Get a clue, will ya?"

Colin didn't seem fazed by what I had said. He just jabbed a fork into some green beans and put them in his mouth. "If we're going to be friends, you can't ever lie to me again," he said as if he hadn't heard me. "We have to be honest with each other all the time." And before I knew what was happening, Colin got up and walked off with his tray.

I watched him hand it off to the cafeteria lady and go into the hall. I put my chin on my fist and tried to figure out what was going on. *Why is he so strange? Why did he act so rude to everybody, including me, and then turn around and talk about being my friend?* I was really curious about him.

While I was thinking all these thoughts, I flipped open my science book. A piece of paper was tucked inside. Oh, brother, that Vicki White had started writing me love notes again! I looked around to make sure nobody was watching and then carefully opened it.

It said, "Watch your back."

CHAPTER THREE

The first day of school ended with dark storm clouds filling the sky and Mr. Felegy whispering something to Mrs. Biedermann right before the bell rang. She frowned as he talked. I figured it had something to do with his breath. Finally, he left and she turned to us with a serious expression on her face.

"Now, children, I don't want you to be alarmed . . ." she started, which automatically alarmed half the girls and Oscar.

Mrs. Biedermann started over. "I don't want you to be alarmed, but we've heard from the state police that there's a *slim* chance—and I mean, *very slim*—that the escaped convict from Connellsville is headed for Odyssey."

The room buzzed with electric whispering.

"We suggest that you call your parents to come pick you up. Or, if you can't do that, be sure to walk home in groups of two or more. Stay in open, public areas. And avoid shortcuts through the woods. How many of you want to call your parents?"

Hands went up all around the room, including Lucy's. Colin was reading a book and didn't look up.

"All right. Follow me," Mrs. Biedermann said as the final bell rang. She took the kids who had raised their hands out of the room and into the hall.

"Don't you wanna call your parents?" Oscar asked as he came up to my desk.

"Nah," I said, shaking my head. "What for?"

"Because the convict might show up!"

"Let him!" I said, grabbing my books and heading for the door. I glanced back at Colin. He didn't move. He was still reading his book.

Oscar caught up to me just before I got outside. "Aren't you afraid?"

"Why should I be? It's just one convict against the two of us. And I took karate."

"So did *I!* We took *one* class at Kim Lee Weinberg's because it was free!" Oscar griped. "Look, let's go back and call my parents."

"We'll be home by the time they get here!" I said.

"But—"

We heard a roll of thunder. I looked up at the charcoal sky as kids poured out of the building and onto the playground. I started walking.

"Jack." Oscar said, following me.

"I wanna go to Whit's End before it rains." I nearly shouted so he could hear me over another roll of thunder.

Oscar grumbled, "All right. But if we run into that convict, I'm gonna have second thoughts about our friendship."

We cut down a couple of side streets, through some backyards, and over a fence that led to an alleyway that would take us to McAlister Park. That was the park in the center of town. Whit's End was on the edge of it. The sky got thick with more clouds, and everything got darker. No sign of the convict, though.

I angled off to a smaller alley between Beatie's Hair Salon and Willard's Liquor Store. It was the kind of alley that dog-legged a couple of times before it opened onto the main street through town. It was always kind of dark, but today, because of the storm, it was darker than usual.

"I don't think we should've come this way," Oscar said.

"You're right," I said.

"I am?" Oscar asked, surprised.

"Yeah. These trash cans smell like booze." And they did. The alley was littered with a couple of large Dumpsters filled to the brim, and there were boxes piled up against the walls of the liquor store. "What a mess! Somebody ought to report this place."

"Maybe we'd better go back," Oscar said.

"Why are you so scared? You think the escaped convict is gonna hang out in a downtown alley where somebody can see him?"

I had just said those words when a stack of boxes fell over right in front of us. Inside the thick cardboard, bottles broke as the boxes hit the ground.

I nearly jumped out of my skin. Oscar shrieked.

"Who's there? Who is it?" he kept saying over and over as he backed away.

A bottle crashed against the wall just behind him, and he leaped forward.

Another bottle shattered on the ground to my right.

I spun around, trying to see where the bottles were coming from. I heard one whiz past my head and break on Beatie's wall.

"Yikes!" Oscar cried out as he dodged another bottle that crashed at his feet.

"Let's get outta here!" I yelled, scrambling toward the end of the alley.

That's when Joe Devlin stepped out from behind a large Dumpster. He had a bottle in his hand, and he laughed in that special way bullies learn in How-to-Be-a-Bully School.

"What a couple of babies!" he said.

"Joe!" Oscar said. I couldn't tell if he was annoyed that it was Joe or relieved that it wasn't the convict after all. To be honest, I didn't think there was much difference between the two.

"You shoulda seen your faces," he sneered. "I thought you guys were gonna have an accident."

"Okay, Joe, real funny," I said. "You had a big laugh. Ha, ha." Then I waved at Oscar and said, "Let's go."

"Wait a minute." Joe stepped in front of me. "Where do

you think you're going? You can't go down this alley without paying the bottle-breaking toll."

"We didn't break any bottles!" Oscar said.

"That's why you have to pay a toll. Now cough up some money or face the consequences!" Joe said with a raised fist wrapped around the neck of a bottle.

"But I don't have any money!" Oscar said.

"Yeah," I added. "You gotta get your timing right. We get our lunch money in the *morning*. Trying to get us after school is a bad idea."

"You're telling me you don't have any money?"

I had three dollars in my pocket, but I wasn't going to admit it. "Bad timing, Joe," I said, hoping it wouldn't count as a lie.

Joe pushed me with his free hand. "Then I guess I'm gonna have to beat one of you up instead," he said.

I tried to figure the odds that I could win in a fight against him. They weren't very good.

"Better watch it, Joe," Oscar said. "Jack knows karate."

"Thanks, Oscar," I mumbled. What a pal! I then tried to figure the odds that I could win in a fight against Joe *and* kill Oscar after it was over. They still weren't very good.

Joe looked interested. "Karate, huh? Then maybe you can show me a few moves while I knock you around."

He tossed the bottle aside; it thudded against a box. Raising his fists, he moved forward. I put down my books and took the karate stance Kim Lee Weinberg had taught me during my free lesson. Joe laughed and swung a fist at me. I dodged it and danced to the side.

"So you're Mr. Fancy Footwork, huh?" Joe threw another punch. I ducked the wrong way, and it grazed my shoulder. "Now we're getting somewhere," he said with a smile.

When I'm really stressed out about something, I sometimes have really crazy thoughts. I did then. I suddenly remembered Mrs. Skelton teaching us in third-grade Sunday-school class that Jesus expected us to turn the other cheek in a fight. I always wondered what Jesus *really* meant by that and if He ever got in a fight when He was my age. Then I wondered what Mrs. Skelton would say if she came down the alley right that minute.

Just then, I thought I heard someone farther down the alley. I stupidly turned my head to see who it was just as Joe threw another punch. His fist hit me on the side of my head—right over my ear. I saw a flash of light—or maybe it was lightning. Either way, it made me lose my balance, and I stumbled into some empty boxes.

Joe was coming in for the kill when suddenly a bottle shattered on the ground between us. At first I figured it came from Joe. But when Joe looked as surprised as I was, I thought maybe Oscar had gotten a shot of bravery and thrown the bottle. But Oscar looked surprised, too. Both of them were looking down the alley. I pulled myself forward on the box where I could see what they saw.

It was Colin. He stood in the middle of the alley with a

bottle in each hand, looking like he was about to have a duel at high noon.

"You can leave now," Colin told Joe.

Joe's nostrils flared angrily. "Oh yeah?" he challenged. "The new kid thinks he's tough. I eat new kids like you for lunch."

"And maybe you can pick your teeth with glass splinters!" Colin said as he hurled another bottle at Joe. This time it crashed on a Dumpster to the right of Joe. At that point, I got the feeling that Colin had *aimed* at the Dumpster—meaning he could have hit Joe if he had meant to.

I think Joe got the same feeling. "You wanna fight? Put down those bottles and fight," he dared Colin.

"I don't wanna fight," Colin said. "I want you to leave my friend alone. And if I have to hit you with a bottle to make you listen, I will."

As if to prove his point, Colin picked up another bottle from one of the cases.

I watched Joe. He looked down, obviously trying to decide if there was a bottle close enough to grab, and even if there was, if he could grab it and throw it at Colin before Colin pulverized him with *his* two bottles. He realized he couldn't, and he began slowly backing away. "Okay, new kid," he said. "I'll give you this one. But it's the last one you get for free."

"Thanks for being so understanding," Colin yelled back as Joe turned on his heels and took off.

Colin walked up to me. I was still hunched on the box. He

held out his hand. I took it, and he pulled me to my feet. Oscar just stood there looking kind of dumbfounded.

"Thanks, Colin," I said.

"Yeah, thanks," Oscar finally said.

"Where are you going?" Colin asked.

"Whit's End. You wanna come?"

"Whit's End? Is that the soda shop place next to the park?"

"Uh huh," I answered. We started walking down the alley. "But it's not just a soda shop, it's—"

Colin cut me off. "I know what Whit's End is."

"You do?" Oscar sounded surprised.

"I've been in town for a couple of weeks. I make it a point to know the area as best I can."

"Really? How come?" Oscar asked.

"Because lives depend on it," he said seriously.

Oscar and I exchanged uneasy looks. I considered asking Colin what he meant, but I knew he'd say it was a secret.

The storm hit just as the three of us climbed the stairs to Whit's End.

CHAPTER FOUR

N eat place," Colin said offhandedly as we walked into Whit's End.

Now, if you've never been there, you need to know that Whit's End is a soda shop like those in old movies. It has a long counter, bright colors, mirrors, old-fashioned straw holders, and all kinds of ice cream. But there's more to it than that. Whit's End is also like a big Victorian house that has all these rooms filled with books and displays and games so that kids can have fun and learn something at the same time. It was created by a man named John Avery Whittaker, who is sometimes called Whit, and is probably the nicest adult I've ever known. He's a big guy with white hair and a white mustache. In fact, I remember in school when we studied a book called *Huckleberry Finn*, I saw a picture of Mark Twain, the man who wrote it. He looked a lot like Mr. Whittaker.

Mr. Whittaker came around the corner and smiled when

he saw us. "Hi, Jack, Oscar," he said. He looked at Colin, and his smile got bigger as he held out his hand for a handshake. "Who's this?" he asked.

"I'm Colin," he said as he stuck out his hand to shake Mr. Whittaker's.

"Hello, Colin," Mr. Whittaker said. "It's nice to meet you. Are you new in Odyssey or just visiting?"

"New, I guess," Colin answered.

"Then welcome to town—and to Whit's End. Jack, you should show him around."

"I was going to," I said.

Oscar took off. "I'm gonna go check out the train set," he said as he disappeared up the stairs.

"If you have any questions about the place, just ask," Mr. Whittaker said, then turned to take care of a customer at the ice cream counter.

I waved for Colin to follow me. "Come on," I said. I figured he might want to see the train set, too, so we headed that way. I thought about asking him what the "Watch your back" note was supposed to mean, but he spoke first.

"Mr. Whittaker's a sharp man," Colin said. "Obviously he likes you a lot."

I agreed, then asked what he meant in particular.

"He pretended not to know me," Colin said.

I didn't get it. "What do you mean he *pretended* not to know you. How could he know you when you just met?"

Colin smiled, and it was the first time I noticed that when

he smiled the corners of his mouth didn't go up like most people's but went down. "I met him the other day when I came in," he said.

"Really?" I said. "Maybe he didn't remember you." But even as I said it, I knew it wasn't true. Mr. Whittaker remembered *everybody*. "Why would he pretend he didn't know you if he does?"

"Probably he didn't want to hurt your feelings," Colin said.

Now I was *really* confused. "What are you talking about?"

Colin stopped just outside the door leading into the train room and turned to me. I could hear the sounds of the trains— the whistles and the metallic skate of the wheels gliding around the tracks. I could even imagine a wide-eyed Oscar leaning over Number 47, trying to make it go as fast as possible without sending it off the side.

Colin had a sad expression on his face. "One thing I've learned is that nobody is what they seem to be," Colin said.

"Huh?"

"People have a reason for what they do. They either want something or they're up to something. But people never do anything just to do it. You can't take anything or anyone at face value. You can't trust anybody." He stopped and looked around suspiciously, then continued, "Like right now, the only reason you asked me to come to Whit's End with you is because I helped you out in the alley. You wouldn't have asked me if we had just bumped into each other on the street, right?"

"Yeah," I had to admit.

"That's called an 'ulterior motive.' It's the reason behind the action," Colin explained. I remembered reading about an ulterior motive in one of my detective novels.

"What's all this have to do with Mr. Whittaker?" I asked.

"Well, I think Mr. Whittaker pretended not to remember me because he felt embarrassed."

"Embarrassed!" I knew that Colin was wrong. Mr. Whittaker never had a reason to be embarrassed.

He went on, "I think he was embarrassed because of what I overheard him saying to Lucy. About *you*."

"Me! They were talking about me?"

"They were talking about how you get yourself in trouble all the time," Colin answered. "Mr. Whittaker said he worried about you. And then Lucy said that the only reason she's friends with you is she feels sorry for you."

"What!" I nearly shouted.

"I'm not finished," Colin said. "She feels sorry for you and then said that your parents asked her to keep an eye on you."

"What's that mean?"

"It sounded to me like she watches you, then reports back to your parents what you do."

I was flabbergasted. It wasn't possible. Lucy, a *spy* for my parents? "I don't believe it," I said. "You didn't hear right."

Colin shrugged and said, "If that's what you wanna believe, go ahead. But I'd check into it if I were you. Does Lucy ever call you when you're not there?"

"Sometimes."

"Then that's probably when she gives your folks the information," Colin said. "It's all a ploy."

I let it sink in for a minute, then shook my head. "No way. Lucy can't be some kind of spy for my parents. It doesn't work like that."

"I heard what I heard," Colin said casually. "You don't have to believe me. But I told you: If we're going to be friends, I'll be completely honest with you. Just see what happens when you get home."

CHAPTER FIVE

The rain had stopped by the time we left Whit's End. Everything outside was wet and had a bluish tint to it. It suited my mood. As much as I didn't want to believe what Colin had said, it stayed on my mind.

Colin took off almost immediately, saying a quick good-bye at the edge of McAlister Park. Oscar and I walked on in silence.

What a day! I thought. *We have an escaped convict sneaking around Odyssey, and now I find out that one of my good friends may be a spy for my parents.* It wasn't like my parents really needed a spy. But the truth was, I sometimes got myself into situations that my parents wouldn't like if they knew about them. Nothing really bad; just kid stuff. But somehow they always found out. Until I talked to Colin, I always figured my parents knew because parents seem to know everything. It was as if they had eyes in the backs of their heads or ESP or something like that. But now . . . now it looked as if they knew everything because Lucy was a secret blabbermouth.

"How come you're so quiet?" Oscar asked.

I shrugged. I didn't want to tell him about my conversation with Colin, just in case he was in on the whole thing, too.

"I saw you and Colin talking about something outside the train room. Did he tell you something?"

"Just the usual stuff," I said.

"*What* usual stuff?" Oscar asked. "You only met him this morning. What kind of stuff could be usual?"

"Never mind!" I snapped at him. "Just quit asking so many questions!"

We didn't say anything else until we got to his house, just down the street from mine. Then it was only "See you tomorrow" and he left me.

I felt bad about snapping at him like that, but it was getting hard for me to know what to say or do. Colin had me all wound up. Maybe he really was wrong about what he'd heard. Maybe he'd misunderstood. *There must be some way to test it*, I thought. As I walked home, I pondered what kind of test would prove or disprove what Colin said. Then I thought of one: I'd wait to see if my parents would say anything about my being sent to the principal's office that morning. They couldn't know unless someone had told them.

I threw open the front door and yelled, "I'm home!"

If Lucy had told my parents about the principal's office, they didn't let on. The time leading up to dinner was as normal as ever. Mom and Dad fixed dinner, talked about their day at work, and got after my little brother, Donald, for leaving a half-eaten bowl of cereal behind the couch in the family room. They didn't ask me about my first day of school at all. That seemed weird. Maybe they were playing *extra* cool to make it seem more casual later. By the time we sat down to dinner, I was certain their strategy was to catch me off guard while I was eating.

After we said grace, Dad reached for the potatoes and said he'd heard that an escaped convict might be in the Odyssey area.

Mom, who works part-time at a bank, said she'd heard the same thing. "I also heard that the schools want kids to call their parents for rides or walk home in small groups just in case the convict was here. Is that right, Jack?" she asked me.

I had a mouth full of pot roast by that time and nodded. I wondered how she had heard.

"Why didn't you call me?" she asked.

I shrugged and tried to say through the food, "I didn't have to. I walked with Oscar. We were safe."

"Don't talk with your mouth full!" Donald squawked. He was five years old and a strict announcer of the house rules. He didn't keep any of them himself, but he made sure everyone else did.

"You probably should have called me anyway," Mom said.

I swallowed my food and tried to sound as normal as possible. "How'd you find out about the school announcement?" I asked. To add to my casual attitude, I picked up my glass of water and took a drink.

"Lucy called for you and mentioned it," Mom said.

I choked on my water and went into heaving gasps.

"That's what you get for talking with your mouth full!" Donald said as Dad slapped me on the back.

"Good grief, Jack!" Dad said. "Be careful!"

"Lucy called?" I asked when I could breathe again.

"Uh huh. Right after school. Probably while you were at Whit's End," she answered.

I remembered that Colin said Lucy probably called saying she wanted to talk to me, then reported to my parents. How tricky! I knew it would just be a matter of time until they would bring up school and nab me about being sent to the principal's office. I glanced at my mom, then my dad, as they ate so casually—as if they didn't know. I never would have given them credit for being such good actors. Then I realized that Donald was staring at me. Did *he* know, too?

"What're you looking at?" I demanded.

"You have a piece of potato on your chin," he answered.

"Oh." I wiped it away, then realized I was being less than cool.

Dinner went on in silence. I knew they were going to bring it up. I knew it. Any second now and they would say something. The more I thought about it, the tighter my stomach got. How would they throw me off guard? Would Mom start clearing the dishes and just *happen* to mention it? No. They would have a better scheme than that. It would come from Dad. Sure! He would clear his throat and, in that low-key voice of his, casually ask how my first day of school went and if anything special happened.

Then Dad cleared his throat. *Here it comes*, I thought.

He pressed his napkin to his lips and tossed it onto the table. "Wonderful meal, darling," he said to Mom.

"Thank you," she said.

He pushed his plate away and leaned forward on the table with his elbows. So masterfully done! Straight out of a movie!

"So . . ." he began, and I knew what he'd say next.

Mom started to pick up the plates. *Both* plans in operation!

"Jack, how was your first day in school, apart from the excitement about the escaped convict?" he asked.

Bells went off in my head. They knew! Lucy had told them! Colin was right!

"Jack? What's wrong?" he asked. All I could do was stare at him.

What a game, I thought. *There he is sitting so normally like he does after every meal, asking me a question for which he already has the answer. What a trick! How should I answer? Should I pretend they don't know, or should I assume they do? Or would it be better to blow Lucy's cover by announcing that I know they already know because of their arrangement with her? Or maybe I should let the game go on?*

"Jack," Mom called as she reached for my plate. "Didn't you hear your dad?"

"You know how my first day was," I said, deciding to blow everything wide open.

"Do I?" Dad asked. He was so cool.

"Yeah. Come on. You know all about it because of your little 'friend.'"

Mom stopped in her tracks on the way to the kitchen with the stack of plates. I must have shocked her with what I knew. She turned to look at me. "Little friend?" she asked.

I laughed knowingly like detectives do in movies. "Okay, if that's how we're gonna play it," I said, talking a lot faster than I meant to. "I got sent to the principal's office 'cause I got in an argument with a new kid and we mouthed off to the teacher."

"Uh oh," Donald said.

"But you guys already knew that 'cause you have spies, right? I didn't have to tell you. Why are you guys spying on me?" Only then did I realize that I was jabbering in a voice that had gone higher than normal.

"Spies!" Mom said as she set the plates down on the table. They clattered on the hard surface. She looked at my dad and said, "Do you know what he's talking about?"

"I think his conscience has gotten the better of him," Dad said, then leaned toward me. "I want to hear more about this, but first I think you'd better change your tone, Jack. I don't like it."

"And I don't like being spied on," I grumbled, looking down at my plate that wasn't there anymore.

"What's gotten into you?" Mom asked.

"I don't understand your attitude," Dad said.

"And I don't understand why you don't trust me. You can just tell Lucy to mind her own business because her cover is blown!"

Mom and Dad looked at me like I was a one-eyed monster who'd just stepped out of a space ship. Dad told me to go to my room until I cooled down.

Okay, I have to confess that the time in my room made me realize I'd played the scene all wrong. I should have waited for them to tell me what they knew before blabbing everything myself. I think I was more nervous than I thought. As it stood, I had no idea whether Colin was right about Lucy's being a spy for my parents. I'd wrecked my own test.

Dad came up later and asked me to tell him the whole story about the principal's office. I did, without saying too much about Colin. I concluded the story with Mr. Felegy letting us off without punishment. Dad said he'd do the same—*this time*. But he warned me not to mouth off to the teacher or Mom and him ever again.

I agreed.

He patted my shoulder and smiled the way he always did when he had to yell at me. "So, do you want to tell me what the nonsense was about spies? Do we have to get stricter about your reading material?"

I shook my head. "It's okay," I said.

"Your imagination got the better of you again?" he asked.

"I guess so."

"You can come back downstairs now if you want to," Dad

said, then left.

I moved over to the window and looked outside. It was dark now, and the rain had started up again. It spat at my window, leaving little drops and ribbonlike trails. Lightning lit up the street like a flash camera taking its picture.

I thought about my parents. I had yelled at them that they didn't trust me. But did I trust *them*? What kind of parents would spy on their own kids? Would my parents really do something like that? I'd known Lucy for a long time. Until I met Colin, I never had a reason not to trust her. But he said that nobody is the way they seem, and we can't really trust *anyone*. To think of Lucy as some kind of tattletale didn't seem right. But how could I know for sure? As I looked into the night, I tried to decide whether Colin was right.

Suddenly, my heart started to race. I jerked my head to look left. For just a moment, I thought I saw something move in the shadows outside. Lightning flashed again, and I was sure I saw a figure standing next to the tree in our neighbor's front yard.

I waited and looked harder. Was it a man? No, too small. A boy? No, maybe it was too big. I wasn't sure. Another flicker of lightning came, but whatever I had seen was gone.

My heart was pounding now. In my mind, I replayed what I thought I'd seen. I was sure it was the escaped convict and he was watching my house. Then, a second later, I replayed the same scene in my imagination and was almost positive that it was someone else. Someone smaller and younger. Someone like Colin.

CHAPTER SIX

So, Jimmy Barclay told Justin Morgan that he heard from Karen Willard that her dad was listening to the police band radio, and they said there was a disturbance in Henry Hecht's garage late last night, and they thought it was the escaped convict trying to get a car or a change of clothes or something like that!"

Oscar was talking in that high-pitched voice he got when he was excited. It was the next day, the day after I'd seen someone in the yard. Oscar and I were having lunch in the school cafeteria. Up until then, it had been a normal kind of day. Everybody was talking about the escaped convict, and I was keeping an eye on Lucy and Colin. Since I didn't know which one I was supposed to trust, I figured it was best to keep my distance from both of them. I don't think either of them noticed.

"We locked all our doors and windows last night. We're not taking any chances!" Oscar said without any sign that he would ever stop talking.

"What makes you think an escaped convict would want to come near your house?" Colin said. As usual, he showed up just in time to make a sharp comment.

Oscar was flustered. "I didn't say he would *want* to come to my house. I just said that . . . Oh, never mind. I think I'll go to the library."

Oscar got up to leave. He looked at me like I was supposed to say something to stop him, but I didn't see any reason I should. It was obvious that Colin made him nervous, so it was probably best that he leave. Besides, I hadn't finished my piece of cardboard apple pie.

Colin sat down, opened his brown lunch bag, pulled out an apple, and took a big, crunchy bite out of it. "You and Oscar been friends a long time?" he asked.

"Since second grade," I answered.

"I guess that means you think you know him real well."

"He's my friend. I guess I know him pretty well."

"Bet you don't know why he keeps going to the library at lunch."

"Bet I do," I said. "He keeps going to the library to get away from *you*."

Colin smiled. "That's probably what he wants you to think, but there's another reason."

"Oh yeah? Like what?"

"He goes there to meet Lucy."

"What do you mean?"

"Did I stutter? He goes there to meet Lucy," Colin said again.

"Why would Oscar go to the library to meet Lucy? That doesn't make sense."

Colin took another bite of his apple. "It makes sense if you can figure out what they're up to."

I rolled my eyes and said, "Yeah, right, like they're up to something."

Colin shrugged.

"What would they be up to?" I asked.

"Who knows?" Colin said. "Maybe they're talking about you. Maybe that's one way Lucy finds out what you're up to so she can tell your parents."

"Aw, cut it out!" I said and angrily tossed my fork onto my tray. "What's with you, anyway? What's the big idea of saying things like that and writing me notes that tell me to watch my back?"

"It's good advice. I told you: Nobody does anything at face value. You can't trust *anyone*."

"Yeah, I know." I pushed my tray away and fixed my eyes on a bright yellow poster that told us to listen to our safety patrols at the crosswalks.

"You don't believe me? Let's go to the library."

"I don't want to," I said.

"Come on," Colin said as he shoved what was left of his apple into his lunch bag. "Let's see if they're in there."

I don't know why I finally said I'd go with him. Colin had

a knack for poking my curiosity just the right way. We walked to the library on the other end of the building.

As we walked, Colin said quietly, "See, you think because I'm the new kid that I don't know anything about these friends of yours that you've known a long time. But I know a lot more than you think. I watch people. I know what they're up to. Everyone has a motive, and once you figure that out, you know how to protect yourself."

"Protect myself from what?"

Colin frowned and said, "Protect yourself so you won't get hurt."

"Yeah? And who hurt you?" I asked.

Colin pressed his lips together. "I can't tell you. Not now."

"I figured you would say that," I said.

"Jack, things are happening right under your nose, and you're too blind to see them." Colin tugged at my arm to keep me from walking into the library. "You don't want them to see you."

He peeked around the doorway. "Uh huh," he said, then stepped back so I could look.

Slowly I leaned forward and glanced into the room. Sure enough, Lucy and Oscar were sitting at one of the tables. Lucy had an open book in front of her, while Oscar leaned forward on his elbows and was talking in that wide-eyed way he did when he was telling secrets.

I took a step back. "So what?" I said. "They're friends. Aren't friends allowed to talk?"

Colin smiled again. "Sure. So I guess you don't care that they might be talking about you."

"No, I don't care," I said, caring *a lot*.

"And I guess you don't care that there are things your best friend, Oscar, hasn't told even *you*," Colin said.

"No, I don't care," I said. "Like what?"

"Take a look at *how* he's talking to her," Colin said.

I peeked in again, but the scene looked the same as it did before. "What about it?" I asked.

"Oscar has a crush on Lucy," Colin said.

"What!" I said too loudly, stumbling back to keep from being seen.

Colin grabbed my arm and dragged me down the hall. "You didn't know, did you?" It wasn't a question; it was an accusation.

"You're crazy," I said. "Oscar doesn't care about girls. And even if he did, he wouldn't like *Lucy*."

"That's what *you* think," Colin said.

"Not a chance," I said.

"Suit yourself," Colin said. "But if I were you, I'd keep a sharp lookout for them. Not only is Lucy blabbing everything to your parents, but Oscar is blabbing everything to Lucy because he likes her."

I shook my head. I couldn't believe it.

"And you have to ask yourself one more thing," Colin said.

"Like what?"

"Ask yourself why Oscar, the guy who is supposed to be

your best friend, has a crush on Lucy and wouldn't tell you."

Everything took a completely different turn after recess. Somebody had been messing around with the desks. Some of the kids started complaining that things were missing from their school boxes and the insides of their desks. My ruler was gone. Lucy complained that some of her colored pens had been taken. Even Colin was missing one of his notebooks.

Mrs. Biedermann got very upset and lectured the entire class about respecting other people's property. For a minute, I thought she was going to cry.

Oscar sent me a note that said, "The escaped convict did it."

I thought, *Sure, the man's running for his life, and out of desperation, he risked being caught to stop by our classroom and pick up essential provisions like my ruler, colored pens, and a notebook.*

Just then Katie Dutton cried out that Joe Devlin had her calculator shoved in his desk.

All eyes went to Joe. He had a very guilty, maybe even panicked, look on his face. Mrs. Biedermann went straight over to him. "Joe, let me see what's in your desk," she demanded.

"It's just a lot of junk!" Joe said.

"Joe," Mrs. Biedermann said so softly that I could barely hear her, but her threatening tone couldn't be missed.

"I don't know where all this stuff came from!" Joe yelled as he pushed his chair back from the desk. "I don't know how it got in here!"

Mrs. Biedermann pulled everything out of Joe's desk. All

the missing things were there.

Nobody was really surprised. We knew nothing was too low for Joe. At one time or another, just about everybody in the class had been teased, picked on, or robbed of their lunch money by Joe. The only thing that didn't make sense was why he'd be so dumb as to steal things and hide them in his desk. I would have given him credit for being smarter than that.

Mrs. Biedermann told us to start our math homework while she personally escorted Joe to the principal's office. I could hear him protesting all the way down the hall.

Across the room, Colin had a funny smile on his face.

CHAPTER SEVEN

Once again, Mrs. Biedermann announced that kids should call home for rides or walk home in groups until the escaped convict was caught. The latest rumor was that he had dressed up like the school janitor and was seen cleaning toilets in the boys' bathroom.

I walked home from school with Oscar, but I felt weird. I wondered if he really was some kind of spy for Lucy. I wondered if Lucy really was a spy for my parents. I wondered if there was really something going between Oscar and Lucy. I wondered why Oscar wouldn't tell me if there was. I wondered why Joe Devlin decided to go on a stealing binge. I wondered a lot of things.

I guess Oscar was wondering some things, too, because he finally said, "What's going on with you?"

"What do you mean?" I asked.

"You're acting very strange," he said.

"I'm not the only one," I answered.

Oscar hung his head. "You were hanging around Colin all day. And you've been avoiding me ever since lunch. Lucy noticed it, too."

"I guess you'd know more about Lucy than I would," I said.

"Huh?"

"Nothing."

"So, how come you're avoiding us?" Oscar asked.

"I'm not avoiding you," I grumbled. "I'm walking with you right now, aren't I?"

"Only because I chased you down. Lucy thinks you're acting weird because of Colin. I think so, too. He's doing something to you."

I rolled my eyes. "Yeah? Like what? Hypnotizing me? You guys are just . . . just jealous because I've made a new friend. Besides, why do you need me when you've gotten so chummy?"

"Who's gotten chummy?"

"You and Lucy."

"What're you talking about? Lucy's always been my friend. Yours, too."

"Oh yeah? Just a friend, huh?"

"Yeah. What're you getting at?"

"Nothing." We walked in silence for minute while I tried to figure out how to ask what I wanted to know. I decided the direct approach wouldn't work, so I'd work up to it another way. I started, "I was just thinking that, you know, maybe two people—a boy and a girl—maybe start out as friends. But after a while, things change, and then those two people—the boy and the girl—start feeling something else, like they do in the movies, and they start meeting in secret places—like the library—so their friends won't find out and tease them or . . . uh . . . you know what I mean."

Oscar looked at me for a long time. I didn't look straight back, but I could see him out of the corner of my eye.

"Wow!" he finally said, barely above a whisper. He had that sound in his voice like you get when you see a great-looking sports car or a large-screen TV.

This is it, I thought. *He's going to tell me he has a crush on Lucy*.

Instead he said, "Jack! Are you telling me you *like* Lucy? Wow!"

"No!" I stopped dead in my tracks and turned to face him. "That's not what I'm telling you!"

"You're not?"

"No! I'm not talking about *me!*"

"Oh. Then *Lucy* has the hots for you?"

"No!"

"Then who has the hots?" He furrowed his brow like he does when he's trying to solve a serious math problem. "I know! Colin has a crush on Lucy."

"Oscar. . . ."

"Lucy has a crush on Colin! No, wait a minute. She said she

doesn't like Colin. Hold on, let me think about this."

I wondered if a whack on the side of the head might snap him out of it, but I decided I'd better not. "Just forget the whole thing," I said and started walking again. "I'm going home."

"Can I come over?"

"Sure," I said, "but Colin's coming over, too. He said he wants to see my baseball card collection."

Oscar looked away and said, "Oh. Never mind. I . . . I have a ton of homework to do."

Colin showed up at my house about an hour later. He looked the same as he did at school—hair combed the same way, clothes and shoes exactly the same. That surprised me. I guess I thought he'd look different sitting on the edge of my bed, in my house, like some adults do when they change out of their work clothes. I remember the time I saw Mr. Felegy at Finneman's Market wearing nothing but an old jogging suit. It looked so weird seeing him without a white shirt and tie. It was embarrassing in a way.

I showed Colin some of my baseball cards. "This is Don Newcombe. He was with the Dodgers. He won the Cy Young Award in 1956."

"Neat," Colin said.

"Did you know that Cy Young had *511* Major League wins?"

"Maybe that's why they named an award after him," Colin said.

"Take a look at these," I said as I flipped through a few

more. "I have Harmon Killebrew and Al Rosen and Mickey Mantle and Roberto Clemente and . . . here's Frank Howard. He was with the Washington Senators."

"Cool," Colin said.

"And this is my favorite because it's really rare," I said proudly as I held up an old, yellowing card my dad had given me. "It belonged to my grandfather. There're only a few left in the world. See? It's Ty Cobb. One of the greatest baseball players ever. Did you know that he was the National League batting champ from 1907 to 1919—except in 1916, when Tris Speaker of Cleveland got it?"

"Can I hold it?" Colin asked.

I handed it to him. "Sure. Just be careful."

Colin looked at the card thoughtfully, then looked up at me. "You didn't believe me, did you?"

"What?"

"You didn't believe me about Oscar and Lucy. Did you ask him? He didn't tell you, did he? I'll bet he dodged the question."

"I . . ." was how I started, but I didn't get any further. Come to think of it, maybe Oscar *did* dodge the question by going through that whole dumb routine of trying to guess who had a crush on whom. Then again, I didn't really come right out and ask him, either. "I don't know what to believe," I said after a while.

Colin shook his head. "You have to trust me on this, Jack. I'm the new kid. I'm an outsider. I've *always* been an outsider no matter where I go, and that lets me see things clearer than you. I've trained myself to watch people and know what they're up to."

"Yeah, I know. That's what you keep saying. And you keep saying you have big secrets, too. So what? I don't understand what the big deal is." I sounded more annoyed than I meant to.

"Okay," Colin said. He stood up, tossed the Ty Cobb card onto my collector's book, and walked over to the window. He looked out just like I had during the storm the night before.

I remembered thinking that I saw someone across the street. Maybe it was the escaped convict. Maybe it was Colin. I thought about asking him if he happened to be in my neighborhood last night, then thought I'd sound crazy if I did.

"We're friends, right?" Colin asked.

The question caught me off guard. I hadn't really thought about it. I guess we had become friends—in a way. So I said yes.

"Then what I'm about to tell you has to be top secret between friends. You can't blab to *anyone —ever*. Have you got it?"

"Sure," I said.

Colin spun around to look at me. "It's a matter of life and death! Do you understand?"

His voice sounded so urgent it worried me. I imagined myself accidentally telling someone Colin's big secret and a dozen people suddenly dying.

"Do you understand?" Colin asked again.

"Yeah, I understand," I answered. The kid was *my* age. What kind of life-or-death secret could he have?

"The reason my family travels so much," he said in a low voice, "is that my dad is in a federal witness-protection program. Do you know what that is?"

I nodded with my mouth hanging open. "It's when the government hides people because they're witnesses against big-time crooks," I said.

"My dad was an accountant who didn't know he was working for a company owned by the Mafia. When he realized it, he got all the files and computer disks with all kinds of evidence and went to the police. They put him in a witness-protection program. *That's* why we move around so much."

"Good grief!" I said. "You mean they move you all over the country so the Mafia can't. . . ."

"Find us and get revenge," Colin said.

No wonder he's such a weird kid, I thought. Suddenly all the pieces fell into place and the bizarre behavior and strange comments made sense. If I were being hidden by the FBI and chased by the Mafia, I wouldn't act very normal either!

"That's only part of it," Colin said and leaned forward on my bed.

"What?" I asked, unable to contain my curiosity.

"The escaped convict is really a hired gun sent by the Mafia to rub out my dad!"

CHAPTER EIGHT

You know the expression about your skin crawling, right? Well, mine did at that moment. It came alive and crawled all over my bones. I'm not kidding.

"The escaped convict is out to . . . to kill your dad?" I gulped.

"Yeah."

"Then why don't you guys get out of here? Why don't they move you again?" I was so upset that I was ready to help them get on a bus right then.

"Calm down, will you? You're getting loud," Colin said.

I quieted down. "Sorry."

"They *did* move my dad. *And* my mom," Colin said.

"Then what are *you* doing here?" I asked.

"The FBI doesn't want me to go back to my parents until they're sure it's safe."

"Then where are you living now?"

He frowned deeply, as if thinking about the answer caused him pain. "You promise you won't tell anybody about any of this?" he asked.

I raised my hand like I was making a pledge. "I promise."

"Because of everything that's going on, I have to live with my aunt and uncle," he said.

I didn't say anything because I could tell Colin wasn't finished.

"They're not very nice people," he said, then looked down at his fingers and started picking at a fingernail.

I waited for more.

"They . . . drink a lot," Colin said softly. "And sometimes they get carried away and . . . they hit me."

I fell back on my bed. "Oh, man!" I said.

I didn't know what else to say or do. I'd heard about things like that. I even remembered rumors about Freddy Zonfeld and how he kept showing up at school with mysterious cuts and bruises and, finally, a broken arm. Some government social agency took him away from his parents.

"I hope you believe me this time," Colin said, "'cause I'm going to be really mad if I told you my deepest secrets and you don't believe me."

"I believe you," I said. "But you can't stay with your aunt and uncle if they're hurting you! Can't you contact the FBI and tell them to get you out of there?"

Colin shook his head. "No, I can't contact them. They have to contact me when they're ready."

I sat up again. "We have to do *something!* Can't you report your aunt and uncle to somebody?"

"I'm afraid that if I do *anything*, it'll cause publicity, and the Mafia will figure out who I am and where I am and then use me as a hostage to make my dad come out of hiding!"

"Good grief!" I said again while my mind felt like it was on overload. All this news was more than I could have imagined.

"Jack!" my mom suddenly called from downstairs.

Colin grabbed my arm. "You can't tell anybody," he insisted. "You promised."

"I promised," I said and went out into the hall. I leaned over the banister, hoping my parents hadn't heard anything and wouldn't ask me any tough questions. "Yeah, Mom?"

She looked up at me from the bottom stair. "Your dad and I decided we should eat out tonight. Pizza sound okay?"

"Yeah!"

"Tell your friend he can come with us if he wants to call his parents and ask."

I went back into my bedroom. Colin was looking at my baseball card collection again. He closed the book and glanced up at me with a question mark in his expression.

"Do you want to have pizza with us?" I asked. "My mom said you can come if you call your aunt and uncle to tell them."

"No, I can't," Colin said. "I'd better go home."

"Aw, come on. Don't you like pizza?"

Colin stood up. "I can't," he said. "I have to go home. Thanks anyway."

"But—"

"I can't, Jack!"

I held up my hands in surrender. "All right already," I said and went back to the stairs. I yelled downstairs that Colin couldn't go out to eat with us.

This time my dad came to the bottom of the stairs. "If he's sure. . . ."

"He's sure," I said.

"Okay. Then come on downstairs and we'll give him a ride home on our way to dinner."

Colin joined me at the banister. "Thank you, Mr. Davis, but I can walk," he said.

"No, you can't," my dad said firmly. "That escaped convict is still on the loose. We're driving you home."

When my dad talked in that tone of voice, nobody but *nobody* could argue with him. We all piled into the car.

*****

Colin lived farther from my house than I had thought. His house was on Mayfair Street in the McAlister Heights section of town. McAlister Heights was where all the rich people lived in houses that were built at the beginning of the century.

"That's the one," Colin said, pointing to a large house with a big porch that wrapped around three sides and seemed to have windows, towers, and chimneys poking out all over.

As Colin got out, I looked around for anything suspicious like an unmarked car from the FBI. All was quiet. The house was dark.

"Thank you for the ride," Colin said. "Good night."

Everybody said good night back to him. He looked at me for a moment as if to silently remind me that I had promised to keep his secret. I nodded at him.

He was walking across the lawn toward the front door when we rounded a corner and I lost sight of him. I leaned my head against the cool car window and thought about everything Colin had said. It gave me a pain in my chest to think of him going home to a drunk aunt or uncle who might knock him around.

"He seems like a nice boy," Mom said.

I tried to think of a way to keep my promise but somehow tell my parents about Colin's aunt and uncle. But I knew I couldn't. It was a matter of life and death, he said.

Dad turned on the radio. Odyssey's all-news station jabbered on. I could barely hear it because of Donald's hand-held computer game. Not that it mattered. We always called it Dad's "boring station."

"Put on some music!" I called out.

"Wait. They're saying something about the escaped convict," Dad said and turned the radio up.

The news announcer was in the middle of a report about the escaped convict's background. I didn't understand much of what he said, but I heard that the convict was a ruffian who had a string of petty crimes on his record until he turned to larger crimes. He was a known thief and a bank robber, but was probably best known as . . . a "runner" for the Mafia.

CHAPTER NINE

Icouldn't sleep that night. My mind wouldn't be quiet. I kept thinking about Oscar having a crush on Lucy and not telling me. Why wouldn't he tell me? Were we friends or not? Maybe not. Maybe the friends I always thought were my friends weren't really my friends after all. How could I consider Lucy my friend when she felt so sorry for me that she became a spy for my parents? What else was going on that I didn't know about? It was as if things were happening right under my nose and I didn't realize it until Colin came along.

Colin. I'd never known anybody like him. He had a dad in the witness-protection program and had to live with an abusive aunt and uncle. What was I supposed to do about him? It seemed like I should be able to help somehow. My parents would know what to do. Mr. Whittaker would have some good advice. But I promised not to tell anyone. And try as I would, I couldn't find a loophole in my promise.

So I tossed and turned until gray light filled my room and the September morning brought a thick, cottonlike feeling to my whole body.

The big news at school was that the escaped convict had *definitely* been seen near Odenton, a little town between Odyssey and Connellsville. And I don't mean seen by somebody's second cousin who had a husband who heard it from somebody who was told by somebody else. I mean it was on the radio and everything. Mrs. Biedermann tried to put a bright face on the news by saying that at least we knew the escaped convict wasn't *in* Odyssey. But Vicki grumbled that Odenton was only a couple of miles away and the escaped convict could have walked to Odyssey by the time the news got around.

It wasn't a good day at school. I felt weird being around Oscar and Lucy. They must have noticed, because they kept their distance from me. They didn't even try to sit with me and Colin at lunch.

We didn't talk about Colin's parents or his aunt and uncle. I guess we both knew it would be a risky thing to do. There was no telling who might overhear us.

I felt lonely. It was like Colin and his secret had put us on an island far away from everybody else. Who could I talk to? It was just Colin and me. And when he left the lunchroom early to finish some math homework he hadn't done the night before, I just played with my food and waited for recess. But recess was no better. I played dodgeball but didn't enjoy it.

Things went from bad to worse when we got back to class

and Vicki complained that somebody had taken money out of her desk. Then Melissa Farmer said someone had taken her grandfather's World War II medal that she had brought in for show and tell. Colin said he was missing his calculator, pens, and a five dollar bill he had hidden in one of his books.

Before anyone could say anything, Joe Devlin jumped to his feet and said he didn't steal anything. Mrs. Biedermann told him to sit down. Instead, he dumped out everything in his desk as if he wanted the satisfaction of doing it before Mrs. Biedermann did. His stuff fell all over the floor, but none of the stolen things were there. I don't think anyone was convinced. Joe could have hidden the stolen things somewhere else.

Poor Mrs. Biedermann. She looked very confused. She lectured us about respecting other people's property again, and she appealed to the thief to return everything that was stolen.

Nobody moved. Nobody breathed. Nobody wanted to do anything suspicious. Robyn Jacobs said that maybe the escaped convict had been sneaking in and stealing things at night.

Mrs. Biedermann quickly said that was unlikely. Then she said she would talk to Mr. Felegy about the "rampant thievery" (that's how she put it). Meanwhile, she wanted us to turn to page 24 in our history books.

*****

The bell rang for school to end, and the normal scramble to get out began. Oscar put on his jacket, grabbed his books, and looked at me nervously.

"I . . . uh . . . can't walk home with you," he said. "My mom's picking me up for a dentist appointment."

"Okay, see ya," I said.

Maybe it was just a coincidence, but Lucy walked out at the same time as Oscar.

Colin was instantly at my elbow. "There they go," he said with a smile.

"Oscar has a dentist appointment," I said in his defense, though I don't know why I felt I had to defend him. Oscar and Lucy probably *were* leaving together. I tried not to care—or to feel left out.

"I can walk part way with you," Colin said. I nodded, and we left.

We talked about the thefts and compared theories. I figured it was Joe Devlin and he'd found a better place to hide the loot.

"I don't think it's Joe," Colin said.

I was surprised. "Why not?"

"I've been watching him, and I can't see when he got into the classroom to steal the stuff. I think it's someone else. Probably someone the teacher trusts to be in the room when no one else is around."

"Like who?" I asked.

Colin shrugged. "Why do I have to figure everything out? *You* think of something for once. Who does the teacher trust?"

I thought about it but couldn't come up with anybody.

"Maybe Robyn?" I finally suggested.

"Maybe. But think harder. Who's probably trusted more than anyone else you know?"

I went through a mental list of everybody I knew. Finally a name came to mind . . . and a face . . . and I refused to believe it.

"Not Lucy," I said.

"Why not?"

"Because Lucy is . . . *Lucy!* She wouldn't do something like that!"

"Yeah, right. Just like she'd never spy on you for your parents," Colin said.

"I . . . I can't believe it," I protested. "Lucy's no thief."

Colin looked at me impatiently. "As far as I can tell, she's the only one who gets in and out of the classroom whenever she wants. She let me in to do my homework during lunch. She's the obvious suspect."

"It can't be her!" I shouted at Colin. Okay, maybe I felt a little stressed out by everything that was going on.

"Are you calling me a liar?"

"No! But maybe you're wrong!"

Colin looked offended. "Have I been wrong about anything so far?"

"I don't know," I said. "I don't know if you're wrong about Lucy *or* Oscar. I don't know if you're right, either." Boy, was I confused.

"After everything I told you, you don't believe me?"

I shook my head "I'm confused, Colin," I said. "I don't

know what to believe anymore. Everything is so strange now . . . but I just can't see Lucy stealing from somebody. It doesn't make sense."

"You don't know what to believe. That means you don't believe *me*," Colin said quietly.

I didn't answer back. I wished we weren't having this conversation. Finally I said, "The only thing I believe is that the escaped convict didn't steal the stuff." I was trying to be funny. It didn't work.

"Okay, I know how to make you believe me," he said. "But you have to promise not to say a word to anybody."

"*Another* promise?" I complained. "I don't think I can make any more promises. Your secrets are too hard."

"I won't tell you unless you promise."

You probably wouldn't have promised. You probably wouldn't have been as curious as I was. But there's something inside of me that kind of tingles when it comes to a good secret, and Colin was a kid with good secrets.

"All right. I promise," I said.

Colin nodded. "Okay. Everybody's trying to figure out where the escaped convict is, right?"

"Right."

"*I* know where he's hiding," Colin said.

"What?"

"I saw him in an abandoned shack on Gower's Field. I'm sure that's where he's been hiding the past couple of days."

My mouth moved up and down a couple of times, but the

words only came out as "No way. You're . . . you're. . . ."

"Wrong?" Colin snapped. "Or maybe I'm lying to you?"

"No. . . ."

"I'm telling you, I know where the escaped convict is hiding! I've been keeping an eye on him."

"Why don't you call the police?" I asked.

"I tried, but they wouldn't believe me because they said I'm a little kid."

"Then get your aunt and uncle to call!"

Colin frowned. "They're never sober enough, and they wouldn't believe me even if they weren't drunk. Besides, if I can watch the escaped convict, I can figure his routine and find a way to catch him. Then my dad will be safe."

I still couldn't believe what I was hearing. "Let's go to my house and tell *my* parents," I offered.

Colin shook his head quickly. "No, you can't," he insisted.

"Why not?"

"Because I want you to see him first."

"I don't wanna see him!" I said. "It's dangerous. We have to tell my parents."

"You *can't* tell your parents. You promised."

I closed my eyes and wished I would learn never ever to make more promises for the rest of my life.

"I'll make a deal with you," Colin said. "You come see him, and if he's still there, *then* we'll call the police. Maybe they'll believe you more than they believed me. Meet me in front of Whit's End at 7:00 tonight. Can you get away from home?"

"I'll try," I said.

"In front of Whit's End at 7:00," he said again, then turned away to walk down the street leading toward his home.

"Wait a minute," I called after him. "Why's it so important that I see him before we tell the police?"

Colin spun around to look at me. "Because then you'll know who and what to believe. You'll believe *me*," he said.

CHAPTER TEN

Wh   hat would you have done if you had been in my
                    shoes?

I walked home and kept repeating over and over
to myself that I promised I wouldn't tell Colin's secrets. But the
three promises were so big that I was afraid I might explode if
I didn't confide in somebody. Who could I talk to? Who could
I make swear to keep the secrets I couldn't keep? Maybe when
we met at Whit's End I could get Colin to talk to Mr. Whittaker
about everything. Mr. Whittaker would know what to do.

I felt nervous and excited at the same time. And that's why
I nearly screamed like a girl when Lucy suddenly stepped out
from behind a tree in my front yard.

"What took you so long?" she asked.

"I got sidetracked," I said and kept walking to the porch.
In my state of mind, I didn't dare talk to her.

"Wait a minute, Jack Davis!" she shouted at me.

I turned around.

"Don't just walk away from me like that. I want to talk to you!" she said.

I bit my tongue and sat down on the bottom step of my front porch. "Yeah?"

Lucy walked up to me. "Yeah! I want to know what's going on here."

"Going on?" I asked, getting sweaty palms.

"I can't figure out what's happening to you." She sat down and looked at me through her big owl-glasses.

"Nothing's happening to me," I said.

"You know that's not true," she said. "You've been acting weird ever since. . . ." She stopped as if she needed to muster up the courage to say it, ". . . ever since you started hanging around with that Colin."

That Colin. What a funny phrase.

She went on, "I thought we were friends. But now I don't know. Even Oscar feels like you've abandoned him."

"*He's* the one who went to the dentist today," I said.

"That's not what I mean and you know it," she fired at me. "How come you're avoiding us? Why don't you want to be our friend anymore? Why are you letting Colin ruin everything?"

Suddenly I felt like I was being ganged up on: Colin with his secrets, Lucy with her accusations. It bugged me. "Don't preach to me about being friends, Lucy. And quit talking about Colin like he did something wrong."

"But he *is* doing something wrong, Jack!" Lucy cried out. "He's trying to tear us apart!"

I denied it.

"Did he tell you we had an argument today?" she asked.

I looked at her, surprised. "No. When did you have an argument?"

"When he came back to class during lunch—to do his homework, he said. I was working on the next issue of the school newspaper and told him he couldn't come into the classroom unless he had Mrs. Biedermann's permission. He got mad and said he was coming in anyway. I said I was going to tell Mrs. Biedermann, and he said, 'You really are a little tattletale, aren't you? Jack said you were.' Did you really tell him I was a tattletale, Jack?"

"No way, Lucy. I never said that," I said while my mind buzzed like a hornet's nest. "Maybe you didn't hear him right."

"I heard him right. He didn't stop there. He told me that you said I was a tattletale and a know-it-all and that you wished we had never become friends in the first place. I didn't believe him, Jack. I knew you wouldn't say things like that."

Hearing her talk like that reminded me of all the reasons I thought she was all right, even though she was a girl. I turned red. Obviously, she believed in me as a friend more than I believed in her.

"I don't get it, Jack," Lucy said. "Why would he say such nasty things?"

I didn't know. "What happened next?" I asked.

"I went to tell Mrs. Biedermann that Colin was in the classroom, but she didn't care. She said Colin was a good student and could do his homework if he needed to. I didn't go back to class until after recess. I didn't want to be in there with him. He gives me the creeps." Lucy stopped for a moment, then said, "I don't understand what's going on."

Everything I learned over the past few days with Colin suddenly went to war inside my head. Nothing made sense. Somebody wasn't telling the truth.

"Talk to me, Jack," Lucy said.

"Look, Lucy, you're telling me all this stuff, but Colin tells me other stuff, and none of it lines up."

"Like what?"

"Like . . . like you and Oscar having secret meetings behind my back," I blurted out.

"What?"

"Go ahead and deny it. You two keep sneaking off together. I was even thinking that maybe Oscar has a crush on you, or you have a crush on him, and neither one of you would tell me." I started fidgeting with the edge of my notebook, bending the thick cardboard back and forth.

"You're such an idiot! Nobody has a crush on anybody," Lucy said, then sighed thoughtfully. "But you're right about the meetings. I won't deny that."

"Aha!" I said. Now maybe she'd confess everything: her spying on me for my parents and. . . .

Lucy looked me dead in the eyes. "The reason Oscar and

I keep having secret meetings is that I'm trying to help Oscar with his reading. He's awful at it. He nearly failed school last year because of it."

"You mean . . . you and he were just reading together? But . . ." I stammered, not sure of what to say next, trying to get it all clear in my brain. "Why didn't he tell me? Why didn't he ask me for help?"

"He was too embarrassed to let anyone know. Even you. And considering the way you've been acting this week, I don't blame him!"

The jab hurt, so I lashed back with "Oh yeah? At least *I'm* not spying on either one of you guys!"

"Spying!"

"Yeah! I guess now you're going to tell me that you haven't been spying on me for my parents!"

Lucy squinted with confusion. "Spying on you? Why would I spy on you?"

"So you can tell my parents what I'm up to!"

Lucy's mouth fell open, and she nearly dropped her girlie pink-and-green knapsack onto the ground. "What?" she shrieked. "Me? Spy on you for your parents? Where did you get such a stupid idea? Why would I do that? Why would your parents *ask* me to do that? Jack Davis, of all the crazy—"

I tried to interrupt, but there was no stopping Lucy once she got started.

"—lamebrained, ridiculous, insane ideas! Even for you, it's a new low!"

"Lucy . . ." I tried again to get a word in edgewise. My suspicions dissolved in front of my eyes. Saying it out loud and hearing her reaction made me realize how crazy it was. But Lucy wasn't going to let me off so easily.

"How, exactly, did you think I was spying on you? Did you think I was carrying secret cameras and video equipment in my knapsack?" For dramatic effect, she unzipped the knapsack and started digging inside as if she might actually pull out a camera. Instead, she started yanking out other things for a mock show and tell. "Maybe a secret microphone in my pencil case? Or a camera in my schoolbook. How about a tape recorder in my lunch bag. . . ."

"Okay, Lucy, you made your point," I said.

"Not so fast, Jack," she said and dug further into the knapsack until she suddenly gasped. Her eyes went so wide they nearly knocked her glasses off. Her face went white. She couldn't take her eyes off something inside the bag.

"What's wrong?"

"I . . . I . . . oh, Jack!" she cried out and handed me her knapsack.

I took it and looked down. There I saw some loose change, a five dollar bill, a calculator, pens . . . and the World War II medal Melissa Farmer brought to school for show and tell.

Lucy's knapsack contained all the things that had been stolen from our classmates.

CHAPTER ELEVEN

I didn't steal any of this stuff! I swear!" Lucy said. Her voice was shrill with panic.

"Then how did it get in your knapsack?" I wondered out loud.

"I don't know! Honest, Jack! My knapsack was hanging in the coat closet. When school was over, I shoved my books in it and left."

"Calm down, Lucy. I believe you. Maybe it's some kind of practical joke. Maybe Joe Devlin did it to—"

"But *why*? Why would he do this?"

"Beats me," I said as I took everything out of the knapsack.

"What am I going to do? If I give it back, everyone will think I was the thief!"

I shook my head. "This is so weird. *Everything* this week has been weird." A new doubt started niggling at the back of my head, but I didn't want to give it a full chance to turn into a real thought.

"We'd better ask your parents," Lucy said anxiously. "They'll know what to do."

"I guess so," I said, then looked over everything that was in the knapsack. It was exactly everything that had been stolen. "Looks like everything's here."

"Oh, Jack, this is awful," Lucy said.

"Don't worry, Lucy. We'll figure something out." I glanced inside the backpack to make sure it was empty. But it wasn't. And the niggling doubt suddenly turned into full-fledged suspicion. I reached into the knapsack and took out a small, flat, rectangular piece of paper.

"Jack?"

Well, it wasn't a piece of paper. It was a bit thicker than a piece of paper.

"Jack, what is that?"

I shook my head and knew beyond a shadow of a doubt that I had gotten it all wrong from the very beginning. Everything I knew to be true, suddenly wasn't anymore. The full-fledged suspicion was now absolutely proved by what I held in my hand.

"Jack! Talk to me! What is that?"

I held up a small, rectangular card, old and yellowing because it had belonged to my grandfather a long time ago and there were only a few left in the world. "It's a baseball card of Ty Cobb," I said. "It's mine. I didn't even know it was missing."

"Did you take it to school?" she asked, baffled by this new

twist and what it might mean.

"No. It was in my bedroom."

"Then how in the world did it get in my knapsack?"

I frowned. I had a knot in my stomach. My world seemed to turn sideways for a second, then turn the other way, then turn back again.

"Only Colin can answer that question," I said.

CHAPTER TWELVE

I t felt like the truth had exploded, and all I could do was
sort through the remains.

If Colin would go so far as to steal my baseball card and
put it in Lucy's knapsack, he must have stolen everything else,
too. And if he was the thief, that made him a liar. So he wasn't
just *wrong* about Lucy and Oscar; he *lied* about what was
going on, trying to pit me against them, or them against me
for reasons I couldn't imagine. Maybe he also lied about his
dad, his aunt and uncle—*everything*.

"You have to tell your parents," Lucy said with finality as
she left.

I nodded. All bets were off. All the promises I made were
based on Colin's lies. I might have been wrong, but I knew that
not talking to my parents was a bigger mistake than keeping
my promises to Colin.

I marched into the house and told my parents everything.

I was surprised by their reaction, or rather their *lack of* reaction. They both looked at me calmly across the kitchen table.

"What possessed you to think we would have someone spy on you?" my mom finally asked. "Don't you think we trust you more than that?"

I hung my head and shrugged.

Then she added, "I really thought you were smarter than that, Jack. To believe a total stranger over your own common sense and experience. . . . What were you thinking?"

Again I shrugged. I felt terrible. "Everything he said sort of made sense," I said. "The way he explained it and everything I saw, all fit together."

Dad put his hand on my arm. "I understand. It's as if his lies had just enough truth to make them believable. That's how it works sometimes."

"Yeah!" I said as my mind ricocheted back to all the conversations Colin and I had ever had. It was almost as if he were playing a game to see how far he could push the truth. I wondered if he goofed up by putting my Ty Cobb baseball card in with the rest of the stolen junk, or if he did it on purpose to see if somebody would catch him.

Dad stood up and went to the phone. "I think his parents should know about this. What's his number?"

"I don't know," I answered, embarrassed. "We always talked at school. He never told me how to call him. I don't even know his parents' names!"

"Or his aunt and uncle—*if* that part was true," Mom said.

Dad dialed information and asked for a phone number for the Francis household in McAlister Heights. The operator said there was nothing listed. Dad hung up and grabbed the phone book, looking at the list of six Francises in Odyssey. He paused for a minute. "I don't want to call all of these folks," he said. "Maybe we should drive to the house where we dropped him off the other night. Let's go, Jack."

*****

"There it is!" I shouted and pointed at the house. Dad pulled over to the curb. The house was dark. We walked up to the front door and pushed the doorbell button. I heard the chimes echo inside. No one came to the door. Dad took a few steps to his right and peeked in the front window.

"The furniture's covered with sheets," Dad said. "Nobody's living here."

"This isn't his house? He told us to drop him off at somebody else's house?" I asked.

"Looks that way," Dad said and turned to go back to the car. "What time did you say you were going to meet him at Whit's End?"

"Seven o'clock."

"Then I guess we should go to Whit's End and hear what Colin has to say for himself."

*****

Mr. Whittaker's normally smiling face was wrinkled into his very-serious-for-important-conversations expression. His bushy eyebrows were bent into a single line. His lips disappeared beneath his thick mustache. But his eyes were bright and moved as if his brain was working overtime because of the story I told.

When I finished, he leaned back into his chair—one of the iron-backed chairs in the soda shop part of Whit's End. He folded his arms and looked at me with concern. "I hope you know now that I would *never* talk about you like that, Jack. And I certainly *didn't* meet Colin until he came in with you. The poor boy obviously has a problem."

Dad agreed, and I tried to imagine what kind of problem a kid would have to make up so many lies.

"It's two minutes past seven," Mr. Whittaker said. "Do you think he'll come?"

I had a feeling he wouldn't. "He probably saw us all here and decided not to come in," I said.

"If I'd given it any thought, we should have hidden and let Jack wait alone. I'm not much of a sleuth," Dad said.

Mr. Whittaker sat forward again. "You were meeting him to go *where*?"

"He was going to take me to see the escaped convict's hideout," I said.

Dad frowned at me. "That's another thing, Jack," he said. "Why would you do something so dangerous? What if he was telling the truth about that? Were you going to leave without telling us? What if something went wrong and the convict caught you?"

"I didn't think about all that stuff," I said, blushing. "I . . . I figured we'd go and sneak a peek and then leave. It doesn't matter now anyway. The whole thing was a lie."

"Was it?" Whit asked. "Are we so sure? What if this was one thing he was telling the truth about?"

"You don't really believe that, do you, Whit?" Dad asked him.

Mr. Whittaker rubbed his mustache thoughtfully. "No way of knowing unless we check. Even if it was a lie, maybe Colin's out there somewhere. He might've created a hideout of some sort to impress Jack. Where was he going to take you?"

"A shack somewhere out at Gower's Field," I answered.

Mr. Whittaker locked up Whit's End, and we left for Gower's Field in our car. I didn't expect to find anything there— not the shack, not the escaped convict, not even Colin.

Boy, was I wrong!

CHAPTER THIRTEEN

Gower's Field was on the north end of town and once belonged to a man named Thaddeus Gower. I once heard somebody say that he was 117 when he died. Now the land belonged to his son Thomas Gower, who looked like he was at least 80 years old. I saw him downtown a couple of times. He never said much to anybody, but he made it clear to the whole town that he didn't mind people on his property as long as they didn't hunt or tear up things.

The field itself stretched out in one direction all the way to the bypass, and in the other direction to Rock Creek. That's a *long* way.

From the backseat, I heard Mr. Whittaker explain to my dad that Mr. Gower only tended the fields right around his house. He didn't bother with the rest of his land. I guess that explained how an escaped convict could hide there and not be seen—*if* he was there at all.

By the time we parked the car beside the dirt road that ran along the south side of the field, Mr. Whittaker remembered that there really was a shack on Gower's property. "It's a shed of some sort," he said as we got out of the car. "If I remember right, we have to go through the woods. It's in a clearing."

Dad found a flashlight in the glove compartment and brought it with us. The drifting clouds blocked out the moon and the stars. The night was pitch black; the woods were even darker. Dad led the way with the flashlight. We had to walk slowly to keep from stumbling.

I don't know about my dad or Mr. Whittaker, but I decided not to talk just in case the escaped convict really was somewhere in the woods. For all I knew, Colin may have set up some kind of trap for us. I didn't know why I thought he'd do such a thing. Then again, I didn't know why he did *any* of the things he did.

It was chilly in the woods, and I wished I had brought a jacket. I also remembered that I hadn't eaten any dinner. With that in mind, I was just imagining one of Mom's barbecued chicken legs when I ran into Mr. Whittaker's back. He and Dad had stopped; I didn't realize until it was too late.

"Sorry," I whispered to Mr. Whittaker.

"It's all right," Mr. Whittaker whispered back. "We've reached a fork in the path."

"Well?" Dad asked Mr. Whittaker. "Which way do we go?"

"I think the path to the right leads to Gower's house. We'd better go left."

"How far is it?" I asked.

"Maybe a half mile. I'm not sure," he answered.

Dad trained the flashlight on the path ahead. "Only one way to find out."

We marched on and on.

I went through my mental checklist again. I was cold, hungry, and tired. Definitely tired. Why did Colin have to make things so difficult? Why did Colin have to pick *me* to be his "friend"—or his victim? I wasn't sure anymore which category I fit into. The whole thing was crazy. There I was, stumbling through some dark woods, looking for a liar, an escaped convict, or *both*, and all because I accidentally knocked books out of some wet-eyed kid's hands. How could I have known? What warning system in my brain should have told me to stay *far* away from that kid?

Dad and Mr. Whittaker suddenly stopped again, and the way they did it told me something was up. I could feel it in the rigid way they stood.

"There it is," Dad said.

"You'd better turn off the flashlight," Mr. Whittaker said.

The flashlight clicked off.

I couldn't see because I was still behind them. I couldn't get around them because of the thick brush on both sides of us. "What's going on?" I asked.

Dad turned sideways so I could see.

Mr. Whittaker was right; there was a clearing up ahead. In the center was a shack. I didn't need the moon or the stars to see it, because there were lights on inside.

"I'm a fool," Mr. Whittaker said. "We never should have done this without calling the police first. I guess I didn't believe anyone would be here."

"Maybe it's just Colin," I said. "Maybe he's trying to play some kind of nasty trick on me."

Dad put his hand on my shoulder. "Maybe he is," he said. "But what if he isn't? What if he told the truth and really saw the escaped convict here?"

We were silent for a minute. I wasn't sure what to do.

"I'm an even bigger fool," Mr. Whittaker said.

"You're not a fool!" I told him.

"Thanks, Jack," he said, "but I have to disagree. I brought us in the long way. If I'd been thinking right, we could've parked along the bypass and walked from there. It's half the distance. Where was my brain?"

"It's all right, Whit," Dad said. "You weren't even sure about the shack until we parked and started walking."

Mr. Whittaker was quiet for a moment, and then he breathed in sharply. "I have an idea," he said. "Holloway's Diner is on that stretch of the bypass. How about if I stay here to keep a lookout while the two of you run there to call the police?"

"Good idea!" Dad said.

*****

Dad and I skirted the edge of the clearing, keeping our eyes on the shack as we passed it at a distance. I was afraid that whoever was in there might see us. Maybe he had a gun. For all I knew, he was watching us with some special night binoculars that let him see in the dark.

Nobody moved inside. The light flickered unsteadily like a candle flame or a lantern. *Just the kind of thing an escaped convict would use*, I thought. *Or a kid like Colin who might be playing a prank.*

Dad and I had circled part of the way around the clearing and the shack when he tugged at my shirt. "This way," he whispered.

I'm not sure how he saw the overgrown path. Maybe it was one of those kinds of things adults have radar about. Somehow we made our way into the woods, getting a safe distance from the shack before Dad turned the flashlight on again. The batteries were wearing down, and it cast a weak, yellow light.

Dad hit the side of the flashlight with the palm of his hand. "I knew I should have checked these batteries," he growled, then sighed. "Lord, please give us some light."

My dad prays a lot. It's important for you to know that. And we pray together as a family, too. It's something my parents think is needed in our house, especially with me as their son, I guess.

Anyway, no sooner did Dad say that than the clouds separated and let the moon shine through. I'll let you figure that one out for yourself.

Dad chuckled, and we walked as quickly as we could down the old path. It was littered with bits of bushes and fallen branches. I did a pretty good job dodging them, but

Dad didn't. And it was a sneaky branch that caught his foot and tripped him.

"Dad!" I cried out louder than I meant to.

"Ouch!" Dad said. He rolled over on his back and drew his ankle up. He touched it gently. "Ouch!"

"What's wrong, Dad? What'd you do?"

Dad pulled himself up to a sitting position and tried to put his foot on the ground. I reached down to help him up. By propping him against a nearby tree, I got him to his feet. He carefully took a step forward.

"Ouch!" he snapped. "No, it's no good. I must have twisted it."

"Lean on me," I said. "We'll make it."

"It'll take too long," Dad said.

"But . . ." I got a knot in my stomach.

Dad leaned toward me. "You go on, son. Run to Holloway's and call the police. Can you do that? Can you give them directions?"

"Sure, Dad, but what about you?" I didn't like this plan at all, but I didn't want to worry him by saying so.

"I'll either try to make my way back to Whit or wait here until the police come."

My heart beat fast.

"Jack?"

I swallowed hard.

"You can do it, Jack. You're like a deer in these woods. Go on."

"But what if . . ." I didn't finish my question because it was too full of what-ifs—like what if I get caught by the escaped convict? Or what if the escaped convict finds you waiting here? Or. . . .

"What if what?" Dad asked.

"What if the police don't believe me?" I asked.

"Make it clear who you are, that you're my son and that Mr. Whittaker is waiting near the shack. Tell them to call your mother if they don't believe you. She'll piece together enough of what's happened to vouch for you. Now, *go*!" he whispered harshly.

I took off, thinking over and over how he said I was like a deer in these woods. I jumped, ducked, dodged, and plowed through the branches, twigs, stones, and thick leaves. With the rhythm of my running, I kept praying that God would let the light of the moon stay just a short while longer.

When my side started to hurt, I slowed down a little and wondered why I was even running. Apart from helping Dad, there was no reason. Colin lied about everything. He lied about the escaped convict being in the shack. I was sure of it. He put that light in the window to trick me. How could I be such a dupe? But Dad needed me to call the police. I picked up my pace to do it.

When I got within hearing distance of the cars and trucks on the bypass, I realized I could hear something else in the woods—the sound of another person running. I hoped it was just the echo of my own feet hitting the ground.

It wasn't.

With a blinding impact that knocked my breath away, somebody tackled me to the ground.

CHAPTER FOURTEEN

You told! You told!" Colin said as he whaled at me with both fists. I was on my back, trying to get some air into my lungs, and was helpless against his punches. Fortunately, he swung wildly and only hit my arms and shoulders. One or two punches connected with my cheek and jaw. But he wasn't very strong.

"Get off!" I shouted when I finally had the strength to push him away. "Are you nuts?"

We both got to our feet at the same time and looked at each other.

"You broke your promises! You betrayed me!" he gasped.

"Yeah? And *you've* been doing nothing but telling lies all along," I said breathlessly.

Colin took a deep breath but never took his eyes off me. "Who said I've been lying?" he challenged.

"You lied about Lucy and Oscar! You lied about Lucy spying on me!"

"I'll bet *she* said so, right? What did you think she'd say? You think she'd admit it?"

I shook my head. "I'm not arguing about it. I'm not playing your game anymore, Colin. I saw all the stolen stuff in her knapsack."

"Aha!" he cried out. But it didn't ring true somehow. "*She* stole everyone's stuff!"

"No, she didn't, and you know it," I said, my voice getting softer. There was no point in yelling. I started to feel sorry for him.

We stayed frozen in place. "What're you talking about?" he asked.

"You stole it, Colin," I said. "You stole everything."

"How can you say that? I thought you were my friend."

"And I thought *you* were *my* friend. You said friends should never lie to each other, but all you've told me are lies. You even stole my Ty Cobb baseball card and put it in Lucy's knapsack. What kind of friend is that?"

His silence told me that his brain was working overtime for an answer. He didn't have one.

"Lucy crossed me up. She didn't like me," he finally said. "She deserved to get the blame for stealing all that junk. I thought Mrs. Biedermann would search everything before we went home. It's too bad she didn't. I would've loved to see the look on Lucy's face when everyone blamed her."

"But . . . *why*, Colin? Why did you tell all those lies and steal and try to make us angry with each other?"

Colin was quiet for a minute. Then: "Like you said, it's a kind of game I like to play to see what people are really made of. You and Lucy and Oscar thought you were such great pals, but all it took was a few words from me and you didn't know what to believe. Some friends you turned out to be!" He laughed, but I knew he was sneering in the darkness.

The light that God had been so nice to give suddenly went out as the moon ducked behind some clouds. I braced myself. I thought Colin might try to jump on me again. He didn't. Instead he nearly blinded me with the beam from a flashlight I didn't know he was carrying. Then, while I was still blinded, he ran off through the woods. For a moment, I watched the light bounce up and down along the trees before it disappeared around a bend. I ran on to Holloway's, but I didn't need to call the police. Three officers were eating dinner there.

*****

Getting back to the shack was a lot easier with the high-powered police flashlights lighting the way. They radioed for backups to come toward the shack from the other direction just in case the escaped convict really was there and tried to run.

I wanted to tell them not to make such a big deal out of it. There was no escaped convict at the shack. I figured my talk with Colin was as close as I would ever get to a confession that he had lied about it all. It was just a game to him, he said.

We approached the shack, and the police officers put their hands on their guns when we saw two men by the door. It was

Dad and Mr. Whittaker.

Two of the officers walked in opposite directions around the shack.

"Dad!" I yelled and ran to him. Boy, was I glad that he was okay!

"Hi, Jack. Good job," he said and gave me a hug.

"Officer Marsh," Mr. Whittaker said to a policeman.

"Hi, Whit . . . Mr. Davis."

"How's your ankle?" I asked Dad.

"Better," he said. "I think it was a minor twist. I just needed to give it some time before I tried to walk on it again."

"Guess I'd better have a look inside the shack," Officer Marsh said.

"Don't bother," I said in my best detective-wrapping-up-the-case voice. "I ran into Colin in the woods before I called you. He lied about everything."

"Really?" Officer Marsh asked.

"That's not entirely accurate," Mr. Whittaker said.

I looked at him, and he obviously saw the puzzled look on my face. He reached inside the door and pulled out bright orange overalls. On the back was stamped in black letters "Connellsville Detention Center."

My jaw hit the floor.

"The escaped convict *was* here," Mr. Whittaker said.

Officer Marsh rushed inside the shack.

I sat down on the ground in shock. In my mind, I could see Colin smiling devilishly.

CHAPTER FIFTEEN

Dad called Mr. Felegy. It seemed he was the only person in Odyssey who knew that Colin and his parents had different last names. Colin's mom was divorced from Colin's dad and was remarried to a man with the last name of Vanderkam. So even if we had called all the Franises in the phone book, we wouldn't have found Colin.

Dad, Mr. Whittaker, and I followed the police cruiser in our car to the Happy Valley Trailer Park not far from Gower's Field. The Vanderkams lived in a long, white trailer that they had tried to make look more like a home by adding a front porch.

Officer Marsh knocked on the front door. Mr. Vanderkam answered it, looking worried when he saw it was a police officer. He invited us all in. Mrs. Vanderkam stepped out from behind the kitchen counter. She began wringing her hands nervously. I thought they both looked really normal, and I felt guilty for barging in on their evening at home. It seemed so calm and peaceful.

"What's wrong?" Mr. Vanderkam asked. They had been watching the news, and now Mrs. Vanderkam rushed to turn down the volume on the tiny TV.

"It's not so much that anything's wrong," Officer Marsh said. "We just need to ask your son a few questions."

Colin's parents exchanged knowing glances.

"Questions about what?" Mrs. Vanderkam asked, still wringing her hands.

Officer Marsh explained about Colin telling me that he saw the escaped convict in the shack at Gower's Field. But the more Mr. and Mrs. Vanderkam asked questions, the more confused Officer Marsh got. Finally Mr. Whittaker suggested that I tell them everything—the lies at school, the lies about his dad being in the witness-protection program and how he lived with his aunt and uncle, the things Colin had stolen from the other kids, and, finally, the events that led up to our going to the escaped convict's hideout. I felt embarrassed telling them the whole story, and I even left out the part where Colin said his aunt and uncle were drunks who abused him.

But then Mrs. Vanderkam asked, "Did he tell you that his aunt and uncle drank a lot and sometimes beat him?"

I blushed.

"Did he? It's all right to say so," she said.

I nodded.

Mr. Vanderkam sighed and said, "It's the same old story."

"What story?" Mr. Whittaker asked. "Has he done this sort

of thing before?"

"Yes," Mrs. Vanderkam said as her eyes got watery.

Mr. Vanderkam jumped in. "Apparently Colin has this fantasy about being the son of a federal witness. I guess he wants a dad who can be a hero in his life. Y'see, his father was the alcoholic who beat both him and his mother. I know Colin has never really liked me, especially after Ruth and I got married. That's when his stories changed and we became the abusive aunt and uncle. I guess it's his way of escaping all the trouble we've had. See, I've been out of work for a long time. It's been hard on all of us."

"Have you tried to get help for him?" my dad asked.

"We tried to get counseling for him, but we had to stop when we moved to Odyssey. We couldn't afford it anymore."

Mr. Whittaker stroked his mustache. "Seems like we should be able to do something about that," he said. And I knew in an instant that Mr. Whittaker would help Colin.

"I'm sorry, folks," Officer Marsh said to Colin's parents, "but I need you and your son to come down to the station anyway."

"I'd be happy to oblige, but Colin isn't here," Mr. Vanderkam said. "He took off earlier this evening, and we don't know where he is."

Officer Marsh looked offended. "You mean you let your son take off without telling you where he's going?" he asked.

"It's not a matter of *letting* him," Mrs. Vanderkam said. "He sneaks out."

"Why don't you call us?" Officer Marsh asked.

Mr. Vanderkam chuckled and said, "If I called you every time he took off without asking, you'd be down here at least five times a week."

Officer Marsh nodded. He had kids of his own.

Just then we heard a car door slam. Officer Marsh frowned, and we followed him through the door. He put his hand on his gun as he realized someone was sitting in the backseat of his police car.

Officer Marsh walked carefully up to the cruiser and threw open the rear passenger-side door. The figure in the backseat leaned into the light. It was Colin.

"I just heard on your radio that they caught the escaped convict from Connellsville," Colin said brightly. "I guess the evidence in the shack helped them figure out where he was headed, huh?"

"Boy," Officer Marsh growled, "you have a lot of explaining to do."

Colin smiled at him, then looked out at the rest of us. "Hi!" he said.

No one answered.

Colin looked straight at me with clear eyes and said, "I'm Colin Francis! Who're you?"

A chill ran up and down my spine. A new game had begun.

*****

Dad, Mr. Whittaker, and I sat at one of the tables at Whit's End. Dad and Mr. Whittaker had coffee. I sipped at my hot chocolate. The nights were cooler now, reminding me that September was awfully close to October, which was awfully close to leaves changing and then wintertime.

"I'm going to be blunt with you, son," Dad began. "Don't you *ever* keep secrets like that from us again. If anyone ever tells you the kinds of things Colin told you, come to us right away. Don't even think twice about it. When I think about his stories of an abusive aunt and uncle and you two sneaking off to look at an escaped convict. . . ." He didn't finish. He just shook his head. "Don't you ever do that again."

I nodded. There was nothing for me to say.

Dad took a drink of his coffee, then added, "It really scares me to think of you spending so much time with such a disturbed boy."

"How was I supposed to know?" I asked.

Dad was quiet for a moment, and then he said, "I guess it's tough at your age to figure out who's your friend and who isn't. Maybe at *any* age."

"One thing you can count on," Mr. Whittaker said. "Anyone who would try to pit you against your other friends probably wouldn't be a good friend to have."

I thought about the things Colin said in the woods. I thought about the way he considered it a victory to show how thin my trust in Oscar and Lucy was. I thought about the way he laughed at me for being so easy to fool. I looked down at my hot chocolate and knew I needed to apologize to both Oscar and Lucy the next day.

Mr. Whittaker touched my arm and spoke as if he had been reading my mind. "Don't feel too bad, Jack," he said. "Colin's a smart kid. Probably *too* smart for his age group. He knew how to sprinkle just enough truth in his lies to fool you."

"He was smart about something else, too," Dad added sadly. "He knew that suspicion breeds suspicion if we let it. Look at the world without any trust in your heart and you'll have to suspect *everyone*. You always have to watch your back. You can never have friends. You can never love."

"What a life!" Mr. Whittaker said. And once again, I knew by that look in his eyes that he would do what he could to help Colin.

"What a terrible life!" my dad said softly, and then he lowered his head like he was praying. Mr. Whittaker did, too.

I sat there with my dad and Mr. Whittaker in a deserted Whit's End and thought about how the place would be packed tomorrow with kids like me having a great time because Mr. Whittaker cared so much about us. I thought about how my mom and dad would keep on loving me even though they were bugged with me for being so stupid. I also thought about Oscar and Lucy, who really were my friends and would stay my friends even after I stumbled all over myself trying to apologize. And for the first time in my life, I thought about how I *could* trust people and believe in them even though kids like Colin might try to make me think otherwise.

What a life! I thought like a prayer of my own. *What a great life!*

About the Author

Paul McCusker is producer, writer, and director for the Adventures in Odyssey audio series. He is also the author of a variety of popular plays including *The First Church of Pete's Garage, Pap's Place*, and co-author of *Sixty-Second Skits* (with Chuck Bolte).

Other Works by the Author

NOVELS:
>*Strange Journey Back* (Focus on the Family)
>*High Flyer with a Flat Tire* (Focus on the Family)
>*The Secret Cave of Robinwood* (Focus on the Family)
>*Behind the Locked Door* (Focus on the Family)
>*Lights Out at Camp What-a-Nut* (Focus on the Family)
>*King's Quest* (Focus on the Family)

INSTRUCTIONAL:
>Youth Ministry Comedy & Drama:
>>*Better Than Bathrobes But Not Quite Broadway*
>>(with Chuck Bolte; Group Books)

PLAYS:
>*Pap's Place* (Lillenas)
>*A Work in Progress* (Lillenas)
>*Snapshots & Portraits* (Lillenas)
>*Camp W* (Contemporary Drama Services)
>*Family Outings* (Lillenas)
>*The Revised Standard Version of Jack Hill* (Baker's Plays)
>*Catacombs* (Lillenas)
>*The Case of the Frozen Saints* (Baker's Plays)
>*The First Church of Pete's Garage* (Baker's Plays)

SKETCH COLLECTIONS:
>*Short Skits for Youth Ministry* (with Chuck Bolte; Group Books)
>*Sixty-Second Skits* (with Chuck Bolte; Group Books)
>*Void Where Prohibited* (Baker's Plays)
>*Fast Food* (Monavah Books)
>*Quick Skits & Discussion Starters* (with Chuck Bolte; Group Books)
>*Vantage Points* (Lillenas)
>*Batteries Not Included* (Baker's Plays)
>*Souvenirs* (Baker's Plays)
>*Sketches of Harvest* (Baker's Plays)

MUSICALS:
>*A Time for Christmas* (Word)
>*Shine the Light of Christmas* (Word)

Other Books by Paul McCusker in the **Adventures in Odyssey® Series**

Strange Journey Back

Mark Prescott hates being a newcomer in the small town of Odyssey. And he's not too thrilled about his only new friend being a girl. That is, until Patti tells him about a time machine called the Imagination Station at Whit's End. Mark is sure he can use the machine to bring his separated parents together again, if only he can get past the time machine's eccentric inventor, John Avery Whittaker. This is a story about friendship, responsibility, and living with change.

High Flyer with a Flat Tire

Joe Devlin is accusing Mark Prescott of slashing the tire on his new bike. Mark didn't do it, but how can he prove his innocence? Only by finding the real culprit! With the help of his wise friend, Whit, Mark untangles the mystery and learns new lessons about friendship and family ties.

The Secret Cave of Robinwood

Mark Prescott promises his friend Patti that he will never reveal the secret of her hidden cave. But when the Israelites, a gang Mark wants to join, are looking for a new clubhouse, Mark thinks of the cave. It would be a perfect place. But he promised. Will he betray the hideaway? Will he risk his friendship with Patti? Mark learns about faithfulness, the need to belong, and the gift of forgiveness.

Behind the Locked Door

Mark Prescott's imagination is going wild. Why does his friend John Avery Whittaker keep his attic door locked? What's hidden up there? While staying with Whit, Mark grows curious when Whit forbids him to go behind the locked door. Mark learns hard lessons about trust, honesty, and the need to guard his thoughts.

Lights Out at Camp What-a-Nut

Mark Prescott is not a happy camper. He went to camp so he could talk with his best friend, Patti. But all she wants to do is talk about her new boyfriend. Then Mark finds out he's in the same cabin with Joe Devlin, Odyssey's biggest bully. Joe gets Mark into trouble with the camp's leaders. Finally, Mark and Joe are paired in a treasure hunt that puts them in unexpected danger. Mark learns about how God uses one person to help another.

The King's Quest

Mark is surprised and upset to find he must move back to Washington, D.C. He feels like running away. And that's exactly what the Imagination Station enables him to do! With Whit's help, he goes on a quest for the king to retrieve a precious ring. Through the journey, Mark faces his fears and learns the importance of obeying authority and striving for eternal things.

Breakaway
With colorful graphics, hot topics and humor, this magazine for teen guys helps them keep their faith on course and gives the latest info on sports, music, celebrities . . . even girls. Best of all, this publication shows teens how they can put their Christian faith into practice and resist peer pressure.

Clubhouse
Here's a fun way to instill Christian principles in your children! With puzzles, easy-to-read stories and exciting activities, Clubhouse provides hours of character-building enjoyment for kids ages 8 to12.

All magazines are published monthly except where otherwise noted. For more information regarding these and other resources, please call Focus on the Family at (719) 531-5181, or write to us at Focus on the Family, Colorado Springs, CO 80995.

You can *hear* more adventures with Jack, Oscar, and Lucy in *Adventures in Odyssey* cassette albums!

Each album contains twelve exciting, family-building episodes on six cassette tapes.

Grins, Grabbers, and Great Getaways
Through the wonder of Whit's storytelling, Jack and Lucy meet Jonah and find themselves dropped in the belly of a whale! Plus a thrilling adventure in 1776 Philadelphia, a mysterious secret room in the basement of Whit's End, and more!

Secrets, Surprises, and Sensational Stories
Rumors abound when Jack's curiosity gets the better of him; a shepherd named David comes face-to-face with a giant named Goliath; we learn about Whit's blind stepmother; and Connie takes a decisive trip to California—plus six more action-packed episodes!

Puns, Parables, and Perilous Predicaments
We learn why Oscar has a problem with reading; Lucy has to make a difficult choice about a class assignment; we hear about "The Boy Who Didn't Go to Church" . . . and more episodes that explore the basics of Christian faith!

Daring Deeds, Sinister Schemes
Lucy is thrown into the middle of a dangerous scheme, Jack and Oscar follow the trail of a mysterious newcomer, and the whole town of Odyssey may be caught in the snares of the evil Dr. Blackgaard! Also includes the popular Imagination Station episode!

Terrific Tales, Mysterious Missions
Jack and Oscar become businessmen, the Imagination Station takes Jack to meet Elijah, Whit leads us on an exciting World War II escapade, and we learn about the secret behind the "Treasure of Le Monde!" Plus six more fantastic episodes!

Don't miss a single Adventure in Odyssey! Listen regularly on the radio! Check local listings or contact Focus on the Family for a program schedule. For more information about other Adventures in Odyssey audiocassettes, compact discs, novels, or videos, call (719) 531-5181, or write to Focus on the Family, Colorado Springs, CO 80995